Stephanie lingered in the kitchen, drinking a glass of juice and watching the vines around the window flutter in the breeze. She thought about Kevin, remembering how handsome he looked when he smiled. He had the nicest blue eyes she had ever seen. But would Kevin ever see her as more than another anonymous sophomore?

The phone rang, and Stephanie hurried to answer it. "Hello?" she said in a polite tone.

"Is Maxine there?"

It was Kevin again! As if on cue, a sleepy-looking Maxine appeared in the doorway.

"It's for you," Stephanie told her. "As usual!" She dropped the phone on the counter in her hurry to get out of the kitchen. Hearing Maxine and Kevin coo at each other was more than she could bear.

Back in her own room, Stephanie pulled her journal out from its hiding place under her mattress and curled up on the bed.

"K.F. is the cutest boy I know," she wrote, "but sometimes he doesn't seem very smart! Why can't he see that Maxine is not his type—and I am?!"

*The SMYTH vs SMITH series*

#1 Oh, Brother!
#2 Stealing the Scene

# Smyth vs Smith 2

## Stealing the Scene

Cheryl Zach

**LYNX BOOKS**
New York

SMYTH VS SMITH #2: STEALING THE SCENE

ISBN: 1-55802-072-1

First Printing/October 1988

This is a work of fiction. Names, characters, places, and incidents are either the product of the author's imagination or are used fictitiously. Any resemblance to actual events, locales, or persons, living or dead, is entirely coincidental.

*Copyright © 1988 by the Jeffrey Weiss Group, Inc.*
All rights reserved. No part of this book may be reproduced or transmitted in any form or by any means electronic or mechanical, including by photocopying, by recording, or by any information storage and retrieval system, without the express written permission of the Publisher, except where permitted by law. For information, contact Lynx Communications, Inc.

This book is published by Lynx Books, a division of Lynx Communications, Inc., 41 Madison Avenue, New York, New York, 10010. The name "Lynx" together with the logotype consisting of a stylized head of a lynx is a trademark of Lynx Communications, Inc.

Printed in the United States of America

0 9 8 7 6 5 4 3 2 1

*For Marcia,
a kindred spirit,
and all the epics we wrote during study hall*

# Smyth vs Smith 2

**Stealing the Scene**

# Chapter One

"This closet must have been designed for a Barbie doll," Maxine Smyth proclaimed in a disgusted voice. Her arms full of blouses and slacks, she peered into the tiny closet which already bulged with clothing.

She had been thrilled when the moving company finally tracked down the wardrobe cartons that had gone astray when Maxine, her brother B.J., and her mother Eve Smyth had moved from Washington, D.C., to their new home in Tampa, Florida. But now that she had her clothing back, where on earth would she put it?

Maxine walked across the hall and looked into the boys' bedroom. "You don't happen to have any empty space in your closet, do you?" she asked.

Hal Smith, sixteen, his brown hair as tousled as usual, was trying to straighten a leaning stack of baseball bats in the corner of the room. "Are you kidding?" he demanded, his almost-six-foot frame towering over the petite Maxine. "I may have to move my *bed* into our closet if B.J. brings in any more sports equipment." The pyramid of bats suddenly collapsed, and Hal quickly jumped out of the way. "See what I mean?"

Maxine grinned. It was true that thirteen-year-old Bill Smyth, Jr., otherwise known as B.J., had enough athletic equipment, trophies, and sports magazines to supply a whole baseball team. His belongings did take up a lot of space in the medium-sized room.

"It's not like I was here first, or anything," Hal murmured.

Maxine's smile faded. "We have to live somewhere," she told him. "Would you like us to camp out with your rabbits in the backyard?"

"Hey, I was just kidding," Hal protested, holding up his hands in defeat.

Maxine ignored his semi-apology and stalked back to her room. Hal, who was her own age, was now officially her stepbrother. Last week his father, Don Smith, had married Maxine and B.J.'s mother, Eve Smyth—now Eve Smith.

"Which means that nobody will ever spell my name properly again," Maxine had said with a sigh. Now she pushed her dark, shoulder-length hair back as she dumped an armload of clothes onto the bed. "And how am I going to manage with a closet the size of a shoe box?"

Just then she saw her mother walk past in the hallway. "Mother! Wait a minute," Maxine called.

Eve Smith, dressed in a comfortable pair of

jeans and a cotton sweater, paused to look into the bedroom. "Yes?"

"I'm never going to get all my clothes into this ridiculous excuse for a closet," Maxine told her. "And what about my bedroom furniture—my brass bed and antique dresser? That isn't going to fit in here, either."

Eve looked around the tiny bedroom, which at the moment held only two twin beds and a small bureau. "I know," she agreed. "This room was adequate for a guest room, but for a full-time bedroom, it is a bit cramped."

"A bit?" Maxine asked.

"You may have to pack up whatever you're not currently wearing and put it away in the attic or garage," Eve said.

Maxine frowned. She looked down at her crisp white slacks and navy and white top, with matching white sandals. How could she keep up her appearance without her full wardrobe? "That's not going to work," Maxine argued. "I can't show up at school looking half-dressed."

"I'm sorry, it's the only thing I can think of at the moment." Eve headed for the kitchen, at the front of the house, leaving Maxine shaking her head at the clothing still piled on the twin beds.

Hal appeared in the doorway. "I'm not sure, but you might be able to put a few things into our closet. I did a little rearranging. Come check it out."

Maxine followed him across the hall to the opposite bedroom. She had to admit that Hal tried to get along most of the time, which was more than could be said for Stephanie, his fifteen-year-old sister. Stephanie couldn't seem to get over her mother's death of three years ago. Since the wedding, she'd spent most of her time ignoring the new members of the family.

Maxine pushed aside the boys' jackets and shirts, hung rather haphazardly on one side of the closet, and looked at the empty space. If they only got rid of the tangle of fishing poles propped up in the corner, she could hang quite a few things at this end.

"You could move those rods and reels into the garage," she pointed out.

Hal looked uncertain. But B.J., who had come into the room just in time to hear his sister's suggestion, reacted strongly.

"What for?" he demanded, wrinkling his freckled nose. As usual, his blond hair was hidden under a faded baseball cap.

"So I can hang some dresses in here," Maxine explained. "I don't have enough room."

"Dresses in *our* closet?" B.J. looked horrified. "Give me a break. Put *your* dumb dresses in the garage!"

"Brothers," Maxine grumbled. They never understood anything. The last thing she needed was another brother. Frowning at them both, she turned back toward her own room.

"Oh, Mom said lunch is ready," B.J. added.

On his way to the kitchen, Hal paused to knock on Stephanie's door. "Lunch, Steph!" he announced.

"Stephanie the hermit," B.J. muttered.

It was true—Stephanie did spend most of her time behind closed doors. What on earth did she do in that bedroom? Maxine wondered. Maybe she was busy reading *War and Peace*. It wasn't as if Stephanie spent any time working on her hair or her face. She seemed to live in tattered cutoffs and her brother's outgrown T-shirts, and the closest she got to makeup was Chap Stick.

Stephanie opened the door and walked down the hall in front of Maxine. With Stephanie's long, thick, reddish hair hanging around her face, Maxine couldn't tell if she was frowning or not, but it was a safe bet. Wasn't she always? Maxine thought, shaking her head.

"What's for lunch?" B.J. asked as they entered the sunny kitchen and took seats around the table.

"How about tuna-fish sandwiches?" Eve stood at the counter, an open can of tuna in her hand.

"Great," Hal answered, sounding pleased. "With mayonnaise and a little chopped pickle mixed in."

"Ugh," Maxine objected. "I hate mayonnaise. I'd like salad dressing, and no pickle."

They frowned at each other from opposite sides of the kitchen table.

Eve took two more cans out of the overhead cabinet and put them on the counter. "I'll make two batches," she promised. "Which kind do you want, B.J.?"

"I hate tuna," he said. "You know that. Can't I have a grilled cheese?"

"I suppose." Eve shrugged. "Get the cheese

out of the refrigerator, please. Stephanie, what about you?"

"I hate sandwiches," Stephanie mumbled.

"Then what would you like?" Eve asked politely.

"Soup, I guess," Stephanie decided. "Don't bother, I'll open a can."

B.J. tossed a package of cheese from the refrigerator over to the counter. "No white bread for me, Mom. Coach always said wheat bread has more vitamins. Pete always eats whole wheat. I wish Pete was here."

"You said that three times at breakfast," Stephanie observed.

B.J. glared at her. "So?"

Maxine thought of their older brother, Pete, who had stayed in Washington with their father, William Smith, a prominent attorney. Pete had wanted to finish his senior year at their old high school, and B.J. was not happy with his decision.

Eve sighed. "Any more requests?"

Maxine decided that someone should help her mother. She stood up and began to pour iced tea into tall glasses.

"I don't want tea," Stephanie said. "I'd rather have lemonade."

"Then you'll have to make a new pitcher," Maxine told her new stepsister sweetly.

Stephanie frowned. "Who drank all the lemonade? The pitcher was half-full this morning." She stared at the two boys.

B.J. shrugged. "It's hot outside," he reminded her. "Can I help it?"

## STEALING THE SCENE

Stephanie looked like she was about to complain, but Eve interrupted by placing a platter of sandwiches between them. "I'll mix some more lemonade in just a minute," she said. "Meanwhile, tuna fish with mayonnaise on this side, with salad dressing on the other. B.J., your grilled cheese is almost ready."

"Can I have two?" B.J. asked. "No, make that three."

Eve nodded. "Two."

Stephanie went to the cupboard and looked at the shelves, then took out a can of soup. She opened the can and poured the soup into a saucepan, waiting till Eve had finished grilling the sandwiches before she moved up to the stove.

*You'd think she's afraid to get too close*, Maxine thought, watching them as she chewed on her sandwich. *What's wrong with Stephanie, anyhow? She couldn't find a nicer stepmother than my mother; why is she so standoffish toward her?*

"Why aren't we waiting for Dad?" Stephanie asked as she brought her bowl of soup to the table. "He always comes home for lunch."

"Not today," Eve said. "He's too busy. He called to say that he'll grab a bite of lunch at the marina."

Stephanie looked unconvinced.

"Don't you remember?" Hal asked her. "Steve, Dad's assistant, quit without any warning. And the marina's always superbusy this time of year."

Stephanie stirred her steaming soup and didn't answer.

Hal added, "I think I'll go down to the marina after lunch and see if I can help out."

B.J. looked up from his second grilled cheese. "I thought we were going to practice some more."

Hal rubbed his right arm. "You wore me out this morning, B.J. I'm not used to tossing baseballs for hours on end."

Maxine watched her younger brother frown. She could guess exactly what he was thinking. *Don't say it*, she thought.

"*Pete* never got tired of helping me practice," B.J. said in an irritated tone.

Maxine winced.

"What a marvel this Pete must be," Stephanie said, looking up from her soup.

"He sure is," B.J. mumbled, stuffing the last quarter of his sandwich into his mouth with one bite and missing her sarcasm completely.

Hal looked a little insulted, but he didn't argue. "Want to come to the marina with me?" he asked B.J. "You've been wanting to see more of it, and the weather's great."

B.J. looked tempted. He glanced at the blue sky through the wide kitchen windows. But he shook his head. "I've got other things to do," he said.

Maxine thought of Don Smith, who seemed anxious to be friends with her brother, and how stubbornly B.J. avoided his new stepfather's company. Both he and Stephanie were having major problems adjusting to their new stepparents, it seemed.

"I need to write to my dad," B.J. told them. "He'll be disappointed if I don't write a letter this week."

Across the table Eve raised her eyebrows in surprise, but didn't comment. Both she and Maxine knew that William Smyth would be more concerned with filing his latest brief than reading a scrawled letter from his youngest son.

"If you say so," Hal agreed. He got up from the table and set his plate and glass in the sink. "I'm going to ride my bike to the marina. See you guys later."

B.J. stood up and headed for his room, and Stephanie slipped out of the kitchen without a word to anyone.

Maxine looked at her mother. "I feel like a porcupine with bad breath," she complained.

Eve grinned. "It's not that bad."

"Yes, it is," Maxine said, too irritated to suppress her grievances any longer. "Stephanie spends all her time in her room, as if she's afraid we might contaminate her, or something. Hal is usually friendly, but most of the time he's either taking care of the rabbits he raises to sell to the pet shop, or working at the marina. B.J.'s grumpy because he misses his friends on the ball team, not to mention Pete—as if we don't! What about all those great vows you two made at the wedding? 'For better or worse'? Where is the *better* part?"

"We won't turn into a real family overnight," Eve said. "Give it some time."

"You said that last week," Maxine mumbled.

Then she looked at her mother more closely. Eve's soft blue eyes appeared tired, and a strand of ash-blond hair had fallen into her face.

Maxine felt a twinge of guilt. "I guess it's not a great way to spend a honeymoon, either," she said, "Don stuck at the marina while you try to make four grumpy teenagers happy."

Eve laughed. "I did accuse Don of hiding out at the marina," she admitted. "But he'll replace his assistant as soon as he can hire someone who's qualified. And don't forget, school starts in two more days."

Maxine didn't know whether to laugh or groan. "A new high school," she said. "I won't know anyone." *But still*, she thought, *entering a new school's got to be easier than coping with this bunch*!

# Chapter Two

Stephanie woke unusually early Monday morning. She opened her eyes slowly and listened to the rush of water in the pipes. Who was taking a shower so early? Hal never got up at this hour. Then she remembered—today was the first day of school!

"Oh, no," Stephanie groaned, rolling over and pulling the pillow over her face.

Unfortunately, hiding her head didn't make the problem go away.

"At least I'm a sophomore this year," Stephanie said aloud, cheering slightly at the thought. "No more lowly-freshman jokes."

She crawled out of bed, leaving the tangled bedcovers untouched, and pulled on a bathrobe. The rushing water had stopped, so she headed for the bathroom. But the door was still closed.

"Hurry up, Hal!" she called.

"What?" Her brother, wearing a knit polo shirt and a new pair of jeans, his brown hair still damp, stuck his head out of his bedroom.

"Who's in the bathroom?" Stephanie demanded.

"I don't know," Hal told her. "I thought B.J. was already out."

"I am," B.J. told them, coming from the opposite end of the hall. "Maxine's in there, making herself *beautiful*." He drew out the last word, grinning at his own joke.

"Hurry up," Stephanie yelled again at the closed door. "I have to shower, too, you know!"

"Breakfast's ready," B.J. told them. Hal nodded, and the two boys headed toward the kitchen. Stephanie followed them.

She figured she might as well eat first; who knew how long Miss Perfect would hog the bathroom?

The good smells in the kitchen cheered her only slightly. Eve was standing in front of the stove, and she smiled at them when they walked in.

"How does French toast and bacon sound?" she asked.

"Terrific," Hal said.

B.J. nodded. "Bring 'em on, I'm starved," he told his mother.

Stephanie slipped into a chair and took a piece of toast from the platter.

"Want some syrup?" Hal asked, offering her the pitcher.

Stephanie shook her head. She got up from the table and went to the pantry, looking through the shelves until she found a jar of honey. Bringing it back to the table, she took a spoonful and spread it over her French toast. Taking a bite of the light, crusty bread, Stephanie thought about the day ahead.

School used to be fun when she was little. But since her mother died, nothing had been the same. Without her mother to tell all the triumphs and disasters of the school day to, Stephanie had lost her enthusiasm for the subjects and pastimes she'd once enjoyed. Her whole life seemed to have dimmed, as if a dark cloud had obscured the sun.

She looked across the table and saw that B.J., despite his claim of overpowering hunger, had only eaten half a piece of toast. He pushed his plate back. "I don't feel so hungry," he said. "Guess I'll get my notebook."

"First-day jitters?" Eve looked sympathetic. "It's almost time to leave. I'll drop you all off in the van, then I'm going over to the marina to help Don in the office."

Stephanie still hadn't gotten into the bathroom. Ready to scream at her stepsister, Stephanie left the rest of her breakfast uneaten and hurried down the hall.

Maxine was just coming out of the bathroom. She wore a red and black jungle-print cotton blouse over a red skirt, with red wooden beads and earrings to match. Her dark hair curved sleekly against her cheek, and her green eyes, subtly accented, looked even larger than usual.

"Other people have to get into the bathroom, you know," Stephanie griped.

Maxine raised one slim brow. "With no mirror

in my bedroom, I have to get ready *some*where," she said.

Stephanie gritted her teeth and hurried into the bathroom. After a whirlwind shower, she toweled her chestnut hair dry, pushed the reddish mass back out of her face—there was no time to make any attempts at styling, even if she knew how—and ran back to her room.

Frowning, she pulled on an old pair of jeans and a faded cotton T-shirt. Eve and Maxine had tried to persuade her to shop for school clothes with them last week, but Stephanie had refused. Somehow she just couldn't bear to wander through the stores alongside the model-perfect Maxine.

"Steph," Hal called. "Van's moving out! Get yourself in gear."

Sighing, Stephanie picked up a notebook, tossed a new pen and pencil into her denim bag, and ran for the doorway.

The drive to Bayview High in the family's new silver-colored van was a short one. Don and Eve had bought the van when it became apparent that the combined Smiths and Smyths simply wouldn't fit in Don's blue sedan.

The first stop was Orange Grove Junior High, which held grades eight and nine.

"I don't see why the ninth graders have to be stuck in the junior high," B.J. grumbled for the tenth time. As he climbed out of the van, he dropped his pencil and had to bend down to retrieve it from the gutter. Several kids on the sidewalk stared at him curiously, and B.J.'s face was red when he straightened up.

"Hang in there, B.J.," Hal murmured. "The first day is rough, but it'll get better."

"I'm okay," B.J. said, his tone gruff.

"Want me to go in with you?" Eve offered.

"Walk in with my *mom*? No way." B.J. sounded appalled by the thought.

"Good luck, then," Eve said.

"See you this afternoon!" Maxine called. "Have fun!"

B.J. squared his shoulders and headed for the school entrance.

Eve pulled the silver van back into the street and they drove on to the high school. When they pulled up in front, Stephanie opened the sliding door and stepped out first. The big brick building looked so intimidating.

"It's bigger than the junior high," she mumbled. "I'll probably get lost."

"Relax," Hal said. He got out and walked beside her, gesturing toward the school. "The auditorium's to the right, two wings of classrooms to the left. You'll get the hang of it real soon."

Maxine, to Stephanie's private disgust, looked perfectly at ease as she crossed the sidewalk and climbed the shallow steps. Two upperclass boys paused at the main entrance to hold the big front doors open for her.

Maxine smiled, murmuring a word of thanks.

"She's going to have them all eating out of her

hand," Stephanie muttered, frowning. The first day of school, and Maxine looked cool and completely poised. What made Maxine so unflappable?

Stephanie looked around for a familiar face, feeling her stomach turn over uncomfortably. She saw a girl from the junior high, but the girl—what was her name?—walked by without meeting Stephanie's glance. So much for old classmates.

Stephanie hurried up the steps and into the wide hallway. She should have called Carol to make sure that her friend remembered to meet her this morning. She hadn't talked to Carol lately, or not as much as she used to. Stephanie wondered if Carol would be her best friend this year, too.

To Stephanie's intense relief, she saw Carol's familiar short, slightly plump figure waiting by the water fountain.

"About time you showed up," Carol said. "It's almost time for the first bell." She had pulled her dark blond hair into a loose knot at the back of her head, and she wore a new oversized cotton sweater and a denim skirt.

Stephanie stared at her friend. "You look awfully stylish all of a sudden. Last year you always wore jeans and T-shirts, like me."

Carol looked down at her own clothes, shrugging. "It's nothing fancy. But we're in high school, now. We're getting old fast, aren't we?" She regarded Stephanie's casual, faded outfit. "Well, some of us anyway."

## STEALING THE SCENE 17

"What's that supposed to mean?" Stephanie demanded. A sudden flare of anger replaced the happiness she'd felt at seeing her friend.

"Nothing, nothing. Come on, we'd better get to class. I hear old Harriman is a real bear if we're late."

Stephanie hurried alongside Carol down the busy hall. A boy jabbed her in the ribs with his elbow as he squeezed past in the opposite direction, and Stephanie winced. Somehow, her first day as a sophomore wasn't getting off to a very good start.

When the first lunch bell rang, Stephanie headed toward the big cafeteria on the first floor. She found Carol waiting just inside the doorway.

"There you are," Carol said. She had put her books in her locker, and carried only a large handbag. "How was advanced English?"

"Not bad," Stephanie answered, looking around the big lunchroom. The roar of student voices, punctuated by the shrill clanging of knives and forks against plastic trays, was almost scary. Lunch had never been Stephanie's favorite part of the school day.

"Come on, let's get in line," Carol said, "or all the good food, at least the edible stuff, will be gone."

They took their places in the long line, while Stephanie looked around her, still searching for familiar faces.

"I saw Kevin Fowler at the marina last week," she informed Carol.

"You mean, your favorite senior hunk." Carol nodded. "Did he speak to you?"

Stephanie frowned at her friend's matter-of-fact question. "Oh, he said hello, but only because he wanted to be introduced to Maxine."

"That's too bad." Carol adjusted the tray in her arms. "You mean, out of all the boys at Bayview, she had to zero in on the one guy you've had a major crush on for over a year?"

"Keep your voice down, I don't want the whole school to know," Stephanie whispered.

When they made it up to the lunch counter, Stephanie picked up a bowl of chili and a fresh pear. She paid for her lunch and waited for Carol to come past the cashier. Then they made their way through the crowded tables, looking for an empty space.

"Over there." Carol nodded toward two seats. "Oh, were you supposed to wait for your sister?"

"My what?" The unfamiliar phrase grated on Stephanie's ears.

"Your stepsister, Maxine, silly."

Stephanie felt a little guilty as she put down her tray and sat at the table. Maxine was all alone in a big new high school. Maybe it would have been a nice thing to do—wait for Maxine so that she didn't have to eat lunch alone.

Glancing up at the doorway, Stephanie saw her stepsister, in her striking red outfit, come through the cafeteria entrance with two equally pretty girls.

"Speak of the devil," Stephanie murmured, nudging Carol.

## STEALING THE SCENE

"So that's Maxine the Great." Carol's eyes widened. "My gosh, she didn't take long to land on her feet, did she? Sarah Anderson and Nicole Taylor are two of the most popular girls in the junior class. What's this stepsister of yours got, anyhow, and where can I buy it?"

"Don't we wish," Stephanie said, her sympathy for Maxine fading fast. "She thinks she's something special, and somehow she makes everyone else think so, too." Stephanie bit into her pear and wiped a drop of juice off her chin. "Forget her."

"Sure," Carol agreed, picking up her roast beef sandwich. "The question is, can you?"

Stephanie refused to watch Maxine any longer. She finished her lunch quickly.

"Let's go down to the girls' lounge before it gets packed," Carol suggested. "My hair's coming down."

"Serves you right for getting so *sophisticated*," Stephanie grinned.

"Hey, don't knock it till you try it," Carol pointed out.

Stephanie didn't answer. She picked up her tray and headed for the disposal chute.

On their way out of the cafeteria, Stephanie spotted a small circle of boys against the far wall.

"Hey, that's Hal," Carol said. "Wait a minute, let's see what he's up to."

They walked closer. Stephanie peered through the circle of students, finally getting a glimpse of her brother. He was demonstrating some of his sleight-of-hand tricks.

Stephanie grinned. Despite Hal's lack of confidence, he had gotten to be a pretty good amateur magician at one time. But she hadn't seen any of his tricks in a while. She stood on tiptoe to watch him pluck a small rubber ball out of another student's ear.

"Hey!" the boy said, startled. "Not bad, Hal."

Hal repeated the trick, making the ball vanish from his palm, then retrieving it from another student's shirt pocket. All the students laughed, and several people applauded.

"Good job, Hal," Stephanie said softly.

Smiling, Hal tried one final trick. He slung his arms wide. Stephanie, who had seen this trick before, knew that the ball should have bounced off the closest student's chest and back into Hal's hand, but something went wrong. Hal lost control of the small rubber ball and it flew through the circle of students.

"Ouch!" a girl's voice exclaimed.

"Uh-oh," Stephanie gulped. That voice was too familiar.

She turned, and sure enough, saw Maxine rubbing her reddened cheek. Maxine's green eyes flashed with anger.

"What's the big idea—throwing a ball in my face?" she demanded.

The circle of students broke up, as the other kids wandered on toward the hallway.

Hal waited, redfaced with embarrassment, to face the angry girl. Stephanie refused to budge, and Carol stood just behind her.

## STEALING THE SCENE

"What do you think you're doing?" Maxine repeated. "You almost took my nose off!"

"Too bad he missed," Stephanie whispered to Carol.

But Maxine, frowning at Hal, didn't seem to notice the two girls. She glared at her stepbrother.

Hal's embarrassment appeared to have tied his tongue into knots. "I didn't mean—I was just—it was an accident," he mumbled.

Maxine looked down at the tile floor; with one foot she rolled the small ball back toward him. "Aren't you a little old to be playing in the cafeteria?" she asked, her tone cold. "Why don't you act your age, for once?"

Hal turned even redder. He seemed to have given up trying to explain. Watching him squirm made Stephanie grit her teeth.

"Who gave *you* the right to tell us what to do?" she snapped. "Did somebody die and make you queen?"

Maxine turned to meet Stephanie's angry glare. "*Someone* has to set an example of mature behavior," she pointed out. "Now, if you'll excuse me, I'm late for French."

To Stephanie's chagrin, Maxine's self-control seemed barely ruffled. She headed toward the hall, where Sarah and Nicole were waiting for her.

Stephanie wanted to stamp her foot, but she refused to give Maxine the chance to call her *childish* again. The nerve of her!

"Sorry," Hal called belatedly after Maxine.

"Don't waste your breath," Stephanie told her brother. "She isn't worth it."

"Wow," Carol said. "I see what you mean."

"I'm going to strangle that girl with my bare hands," Stephanie promised. "Probably before the week's out!"

# Chapter Three

Maxine's face stung for minutes after Hal's ball struck her, and her eyes teared from the pain of the unexpected blow. Blinking, she rubbed her cheek as she hurried off to class beside Sarah and Nicole.

*What a dumb thing to do*, she said to herself. Tossing a ball around in the cafeteria. Didn't a sixteen-year-old boy have better things to do with his time?

"Okay, this is your room," Sarah told her. "See you later, Maxine."

"Thanks," Maxine said. She walked through the doorway and found a seat in the classroom. As she sat down at the desk, she rubbed her face one last time. The soreness was finally going away.

The teacher in the front of the room began talking, and Maxine tried to concentrate. But a picture of Hal's contrite face kept coming to her mind, and she couldn't push it away. Okay, maybe she had been a little hard on Hal, though he should have been more careful. And maybe she had overreacted.

It *was* her first day in a new school. No matter how well she disguised it, she was still aware of the tension that was making her whole body stiff. No one else might notice, but the anxiety was there. Maxine took a deep breath, trying to relax her shoulders and neck—they felt as if they were soldered with solid steel.

It could have been much worse. She'd been really lucky to meet two nice girls during her morning classes. Sarah and Nicole were both well dressed, intelligent, and poised—the kind of girls Maxine was automatically attracted to. It was too early to tell if they would be good friends, but Maxine was pleased, nonetheless.

She looked around the French class to see if she recognized any faces. A blond-haired girl who looked familiar was staring at her.

Maxine smiled. "Tina, right? I met you at Mom and Don's wedding."

Tina nodded. "What do you think of Bayview?"

"It's a nice school." Maxine replied. "I think I'm going to like it here."

"It's pretty big, of course," Tina said, her tone slightly patronizing. "But you'll get used to it pretty soon, I'm sure."

Maxine smiled, resisting the impulse to tell the other girl that her last high school in Washington, D.C. hadn't been exactly small.

"*Attention, s'il vous plaît*," the teacher said,

## STEALING THE SCENE 25

clapping his hands together. Maxine and Tina both turned their heads toward the front of the room.

"Do you need any help finding your next class?" Tina asked as she and Maxine walked out of the classroom. "I'm on my way to drama, but I can give you directions."

"I'm going that way, too," Maxine said. "In fact, that's my next class."

"Drama two?" Tina looked surprised. "Are you sure? That's the advanced class, you know."

Maxine nodded. She'd been waiting for this class all day. The drama classroom was a large room near the auditorium, convenient to the stage area—she had already checked its location. She and Tina walked down the hall and into the big room, and Maxine looked around with real interest.

There were old flats—canvas backdrops left over from other plays—propped against the back wall. One closet was labeled Costumes, and a large cabinet contained makeup supplies. Maxine could hardly wait to explore all the resources.

A short, red-haired boy stood in the center of the group of students, talking to Georgette McDivott, another girl Maxine had met at her mother's wedding. He paused when Maxine and Tina came into the room.

"Hi," he said. "New student? I'm Jake, fellow thespian."

Maxine smiled. "I'm Maxine, brand-new

Tampa resident," she told him. "Hello again, Georgette."

Georgette looked just as surprised to see Maxine in the advanced class as her friend Tina had been, and not very pleased, either. "Hi. You're in drama two? This class has a prerequisite, and Mrs. Mundy personally selects the students allowed to enroll, you know."

"I know," Maxine replied. "I went through it all with the guidance counselor when I registered last week. I've already had beginning drama, so they let me enroll, subject to Mrs. Mundy's approval."

Georgette's expression relaxed. "She's pretty demanding, so don't be too disappointed if she makes you drop back to the beginner's group. Oh, here she is now."

They all turned to watch the teacher come through the doorway. Mrs. Mundy was a small woman, but she walked with a theatrical flourish, wearing a black knit top and a long skirt in a wild purple and scarlet print, with a red scarf flung artfully over her shoulder. Her red hair curled wildly about her small face, and her make up was startling. But her eyes were bright with intelligence and humor, and Maxine felt sure she was going to enjoy this class.

"Well, class," Mrs. Mundy greeted them. Her voice was unexpectedly deep, and she used it to full advantage to get everyone's attention. "Everyone present and ready to start work on our first play?"

"We can't wait, Mrs. Mundy," Tina told her.

"We've thought of nothing else for the last month. What is it going to be?"

"*A Midsummer Night's Dream*," the teacher said. "The Bard himself."

Some of the girls looked pleased, but Jake groaned. "More Shakespeare? I thought doing *Twelfth Night* last year was bad enough."

"Now, now," Mrs. Mundy admonished, grinning. "Any actor worth his salt likes to tackle the master again and again. We'll begin tryouts Wednesday afternoon after school. I'll have announcements posted around the school tomorrow morning."

As the rest of the class began to settle into the desks that formed a semicircle, Mrs. Mundy dropped a big canvas carry-all bag on the desktop. She gestured impatiently at the stack of textbooks in front of her.

"Georgette, please start distributing the books for me. Who are you—a new student?" she asked, suddenly noticing Maxine.

"I'm Maxine Smyth, Mrs. Mundy. I just transferred from Washington, D.C. My records haven't arrived yet, but I've taken a year of drama already, and two years of speech."

"I see." Mrs. Mundy looked her over appraisingly. "Any stage experience?"

Maxine nodded and began to list the roles she'd played at her old school. The drama teacher nodded in approval. "Sounds like you've had enough background for this class," Mrs. Mundy told her. "Planning to try out Wednesday? You're not intimidated by Shakespeare, are you?"

"Oh, no," Maxine assured her. "I mean, yes, I do want to try out, very much."

"Fine." Mrs. Mundy nodded. "Some new blood will do our little group good. I've some promising faces in my beginning drama class, too, so we should have a wide field to choose from."

From the corner of her eye, Maxine saw that Georgette and Tina were looking at her with expressions of marked dismay. They didn't seem eager to welcome a new student to advanced drama.

Mrs. Mundy dug her roll book out of her carryall bag and began to check off the names of the students.

Maxine found a desk and sat down, her mind on the upcoming tryouts. She could feel her heart beat faster just thinking about Wednesday. *Please, please let me do well enough to get a part,* she thought.

Maxine paid close attention to Mrs. Mundy's introduction to the class, and looked through the textbook with interest. After the teacher concluded her remarks, she assigned a chapter to read for the next day. Several people opened their books, while some of the other students talked quietly to each other. Mrs. Mundy didn't appear to mind, but Maxine was too absorbed in her own thoughts to be interested in the conversations around her. If she wanted a good part in the play, there was only one thing to do: read and practice it before Wednesday.

When the bell rang, Maxine hurried upstairs to

the library. She quickly found the drama section, but discovered that others must have had the same idea. There were no more copies of *A Midsummer Night's Dream* left on the shelf.

Walking back past the main desk, she saw Georgette holding two slim volumes of the play. "I guess we had the same plan," Maxine said nicely.

The other girl shrugged. "I've never read this play," she admitted. "I wanted to study it before the tryouts."

Maxine smiled, trying not to look too disappointed. "You must have picked up the last two copies."

"Oh?" Georgette didn't quite meet her gaze. "I'd let you have one of these, but I promised Tina I'd get a copy for her. Anyhow, as established members of the drama group, I think we have seniority, or something like that."

"Maybe," Maxine said, hiding her anger from Georgette. How could she be so unfriendly? she wondered. "I'll see you later." Maxine left without waiting for a reply and walked down the wide staircase and out through the main entrance.

The mob of students in front of the school made her pause for a minute. But Hal had outlined the bus schedule for her that morning, so she walked along the front of the school until she spotted the line of yellow buses on the side.

"Maxine?"

Maxine turned around. Kevin Fowler, a senior she'd briefly met at Don Smith's marina, stood a few feet away, smiling. He was very cute, she thought, with his intense blue eyes and wavy blond hair. "Hello—Kevin, right?"

"Right. I looked for you all day, but I just couldn't seem to catch up with you. How was your first day at Bayview?"

"Not bad," Maxine told him. "I was just looking for the right bus." She couldn't help feeling excited by the fact that Kevin had remembered her, and—with all the girls in the high school to choose from—had made a point of searching for her.

"Well, would you like a ride home?" Kevin asked. "I have my car here, and I'd be glad to drop you off."

Maxine smiled shyly. She didn't want to show Kevin just how pleased she was with his offer—boys liked a bit of a challenge, after all. But to start a new school year with a hunk like Kevin seeking her company—Maxine felt better and better about this high school. Kevin seemed really sweet.

"Terrific. Hold on for a second—I want to tell Hal or Stephanie so they don't think I missed the bus, okay?"

"Sure. I'll wait for you up at the corner."

Maxine walked quickly toward the buses. She recognized Stephanie's familiar faded T-shirt as the other girl started to board the bus.

"Wait a minute, Stephanie!" Maxine called.

Stephanie looked over her shoulder. "Oh, it's you," she said. "This is our bus."

"I know that," Maxine said, "but I've got a ride home. Will you tell Mom I'll be there soon?"

## STEALING THE SCENE

"You have a ride?" Stephanie stared at her stepsister in apparent surprise. "With who?"

"With whom," Maxine corrected her. "With Kevin Fowler. The boy we saw at the marina a couple of weeks ago, remember?"

Stephanie's expression looked a bit strange. "I remember," she blurted, and seemed about to add something else.

Maxine waited, but Stephanie only frowned fiercely. "Why are you going with him?"

"Because he asked me," Maxine told her. "I think he's nice. Don't you like him?"

Stephanie chewed on her lower lip. "He's all right. Guess I'd better get on the bus," she muttered.

"Right," Maxine nodded. "Don't forget to tell Mom."

Leaving Stephanie to climb on the bus, Maxine walked back up the grassy incline toward the spot where Kevin waited. He was very good-looking, she thought, noticing the broad shoulders beneath his cotton shirt. They would make a good couple—they both dressed well. Then she remembered her mission for the afternoon.

"Do you know if there's a bookstore nearby?" Maxine asked Kevin.

He nodded. "Sure, there's one not too far away. Cramming already?"

"You might say that." Maxine smiled. "Would you mind stopping by there before you take me home?"

"No problem," Kevin assured her. "Maybe we'll splurge on an ice-cream cone while we're at the shopping center. No rush to get you home, is there?"

"Not at all." Maxine and Kevin walked side by side through the parking lot to his car.

"So how do you like Bayview High?" Kevin asked as he unlocked his small red sedan.

"It's okay. I only have one complaint," she said, getting into the passenger seat.

"What's that?"

She loved the way his sandy eyebrows rose when he looked at her.

"The name of the place. I don't believe you can actually *see* the bay from this school."

Kevin grinned, turning the key in the ignition. The engine sputtered to life, then hummed smoothly as he changed gears. "Sure you can," he argued. "All you have to do is stand on a ladder on the highest part of the roof!"

Maxine giggled, and the little car pulled into the street.

# Chapter Four

Maxine located a copy of *A Midsummer Night's Dream* at the bookstore in the shopping center. Kevin waited while she paid for the paperback, then they walked along the storefronts until they came to a small ice-cream bar.

Inside, there were small white tables with white stools, and red banners hanging over the counter. Maxine looked through the glass fronts at the vats of ice cream. It was hard to choose, but she finally picked a flavor, and they selected a table and sat down. She told Kevin about her plans to audition on Wednesday.

"You're really excited about this, aren't you?" Kevin said.

Maxine nodded. "I've always loved acting," she told him. "There's something really exciting about being onstage. I love to get into a role, pretend to be someone else entirely." She took another lick of her scoop of pralines and cream.

"Isn't that hard to do?" Kevin asked, swallowing a big bite of ice cream. He had ordered a tall triple scoop of chocolate fudge, which was rapidly disappearing. "The only role I ever played was a frog in my kindergarten's spring pageant. And I wasn't the only one!"

Maxine grinned. "It's not so tough. You sort of let go of yourself and take on a new identity. Then I can do tons of things I would never do myself. I've always wanted to try Lady Macbeth."

Kevin shook his head. "I think I'll stick to sailing," he said, crunching the top of his cone. "That's something a little more mellow. Speaking of which . . . would you like to go for a sail in my boat on Saturday?"

Maxine concentrated on her cone for a moment. Her one visit to the marina hadn't exactly overwhelmed her. On the other hand, she was certainly bound to have more fun with Kevin than she had with Stephanie.

"Sure. I'll warn you, though—I've never been out in a small boat." Maxine admitted. "But if you don't mind a total beginner on board, we're on."

"Great! Don't worry, you'll catch on quickly. And I know you'll love it. You haven't lived till you've skimmed over the bay on a brisk day, with blue skies overhead and the wind at your back!"

He continued to talk about his sailboat, sometimes throwing in technical terms that Maxine didn't understand. But she smiled into his blue eyes while he rushed on, content to let him talk while her thoughts drifted back to the tryouts.

Later, when they pulled into the Smith driveway, Maxine thanked him again for the ride.

"Just call me the Welcome Wagon. I'll see you tomorrow," Kevin said. He hesitated a moment, as if debating whether to lean forward and give Maxine a quick kiss. But instead, he just grinned at her.

Maxine nodded. "You bet," she agreed, slipping out of the car and waving as he pulled away. She felt both disappointed and relieved that he hadn't kissed her. She liked him a lot, but she wasn't eager to rush into anything.

With her books under one arm, Maxine walked into the house.

She saw Stephanie in the kitchen, sitting in front of the window, licking peanut butter off a large spoon.

"Have a good day at school?" Maxine asked, trying to be pleasant.

Stephanie, instead of answering, turned and hurried down the hall.

Maxine heard the bedroom door slam. "What did I do now?" she muttered to herself.

Putting her books on the counter, Maxine poured herself a glass of iced tea. Where was everyone? She wandered out to the backyard and discovered the two boys. Hal was in the rabbit pen; B.J., looking moody, was tossing a baseball up in the air.

"How was school?" Maxine asked her younger brother.

"That junior high is a zoo." B.J. frowned. "I went to the wrong class twice."

Maxine giggled, but she patted him on the shoulder. "You'll get used to it, trust me."

"Maybe," B.J. said. "But there's a lot of big guys around, Maxine. I don't know, I think I'd be better off back in D.C."

"Translation?" Maxine lifted her brows.

"What if I don't make the baseball team?" B.J. said. "What if I'm not good enough?"

"Relax," Maxine said. "You're a good player, you know you are. Anyhow, all you can do is give it your best shot. Worrying won't help."

"I've really got to practice," B.J. muttered. "I don't have anyone to throw the ball to."

Hal looked around. "Come on, B.J. I practiced with you for almost an hour. I've got to get the rabbit pen cleaned and the animals fed before dinner." He went back to his raking.

B.J. made a face. "If Pete were here, I'd have someone to coach me," he complained. "Hal can catch a ball, but he doesn't know much about the finer points of the game."

Maxine couldn't help laughing. "Like me, huh?"

"Well, you're just a girl," B.J. told her generously. "But I need someone who knows what he's doing."

Maxine, watching B.J.'s glum expression, tried to cheer him up. "If it's any help, I'll catch for you, B.J."

"I guess you're better than nothing," her brother muttered. "Here, take Hal's glove and stand at the corner of the yard."

"Hold on, I want to change first. I'll be right back," Maxine promised. Running into the house, she braced herself in anticipation of fielding B.J.'s powerful pitches. She hoped she wouldn't break all her nails.

It was some time later before Eve called them to dinner, but Maxine was happy to be released from baseball duty. They all went inside and washed up, then joined Don and Eve at the table. Stephanie had finally emerged from her room, though she still didn't seem very talkative.

"How was school?" Eve asked as she spooned savory-smelling tomato sauce over plates of spaghetti.

"Not bad," Hal said, taking a large portion. "Boy, this smells good. We haven't had dinners like these in ages."

Stephanie threw her brother a dark look.

"Not that Stephanie didn't do a good job in the kitchen," Hal added hastily. "And school was okay. My classes seem pretty interesting."

"Do you and Maxine have any classes together?" Don passed around a large bowl of tossed salad. "You're both juniors."

Hal nodded. "Advanced English and American history," he said.

Maxine looked up. She had, in fact, been surprised to find Hal in her advanced classes. She hadn't realized that her stepbrother was an above-average student. Still, a familiar face was always welcome. Then she remembered the incident in the cafeteria, and silently added, *as long as he doesn't try any more magic tricks*!

Meanwhile, B.J. was telling his mother about his worries. "What if I don't make the ball team?" he said.

"I'm sure you have a good chance," Eve tried to reassure him. "You didn't have any trouble making the team last year."

"But this is a whole different school," B.J. pointed out. "And I don't have Pete here to coach me."

Don looked up from his dinner. "I'll be glad to help you practice, B.J., as soon as I hire someone new at the marina so I have a little free time."

B.J. looked at his stepfather, his expression almost suspicious. "Did you play baseball in high school?"

"Well, not on the team," Don admitted. "But I played with my friends."

B.J. didn't look impressed. "My father was a district champion in high school," he muttered as he took another bite of spaghetti.

There was a short silence around the table. "Everyone has his own strengths," Eve said gently.

Meanwhile, Stephanie had finished her salad and was picking suspiciously at the spaghetti on her plate. "Are there onions in this sauce?"

Eve nodded.

"I hate onions," Stephanie said, pushing her plate away.

Eve said, "I'm sorry, I didn't know that. Next time, I'll omit the onions from my recipe."

B.J. looked up in alarm. "Hey, it won't be good without the onions."

"Then I'll make *two* batches," Eve told them, sounding tired.

"Try the spaghetti, Stephanie," Don said. "It's delicious."

"I'm not very hungry, anyhow," Stephanie said. She got up from the table.

*Oh boy*, Maxine thought. *Here we go again.* It seemed like a good time to change the subject.

"Guess what," she said enthusiastically. "Tryouts for the first school play are Wednesday afternoon! Mrs. Mundy, the drama teacher, is producing *A Midsummer Night's Dream*."

"Which part are you going to try out for?" Don asked.

"Whichever role I think I have the best chance for," Maxine told them. "I'm not picky. I mean, a big part would be great, but the most important thing is being in the play, period."

"That sounds like a fun play to work on," Eve said. She picked up a bowl of fresh fruit and passed it around the table. Maxine ate a few grapes, then stood up and collected the dirty plates.

"Want me to stack the dishes in the dishwasher?" she offered.

"Go ahead and start your homework," Don told her. "I'll give your mother a hand. She's been working at the marina all day."

The two boys disappeared from the kitchen without any persuasion, and Maxine went back to her small room, taking her books and curling up on one of the twin beds. But it was hard to concentrate on her literature assignment; she was more anxious to read the play and start rehearsing.

On Wednesday afternoon Maxine hurried to the auditorium right after school. The past two days had seemed to last an eternity, but the time for tryouts had finally arrived. To her chagrin, she found a large crowd of students already assembled.

Were all these people auditioning? And how many of them had already worked with Mrs. Mundy and given performances in the past that might sway the drama teacher to award them big roles?

Feeling distinctly discouraged, Maxine sat down in one of the seats at the back of the auditorium.

She saw Georgette and Tina sitting in the front, along with Jake and other students from Drama Two whose names she didn't know.

Mrs. Mundy called the assembly to order. "Quiet, please! Everyone please sign in on my list, so I don't leave anyone out accidentally. We'll get started right away, because this may take a while." She started passing her clipboard with a blank sheet of paper through the crowd of students.

When the clipboard finally made its way back

# STEALING THE SCENE 41

to Maxine, she signed her name, and, under Part Reading For wrote Titania. This was the role of Queen of the Fairies—not the lead role, but a good part. Maxine was afraid to set her sights too high for her first audition with a new drama teacher.

*Better to get a small part*, she told herself, *than to be left out and not be a part of the production at all.* If worse came to worst, maybe Mrs. Mundy would cast her as one of the fairies. Those parts were small, but it would give her a chance to work and learn.

Despite this decision, Maxine felt herself grow tense as she waited for her turn to read. A number of students hadn't bothered to check out the play ahead of time, and their readings were awkward as they fumbled through the unfamiliar Shakespearean syntax. But several gave very polished performances. Maxine noted a tall, blond girl in particular who seemed very good. Her name was Anne, and Maxine was sure she'd end up in a lead role.

"How's it going?" someone whispered from behind her.

Maxine looked over her shoulder and saw Hal grinning at her.

"What are you doing here?" she demanded. "You're not going to throw something at me, are you?"

Hal looked offended. "Come on, aren't you ever going to let me forget that? I just came by to wish you luck."

"*Shhh*," someone in front hissed at them.

Hal lowered his voice, but he went on stubbornly, "I just wanted to help."

"Then leave me alone," Maxine told him. "I'm nervous enough by myself!"

She felt bad for being so mean, but she was too keyed up to deal with more distractions. And Hal always seemed to attract accidents. She didn't need anything unexpected destroying her concentration. She stared back down at her copy of the play, willing him to go away.

The next time she looked up, Hal, his mouth set stubbornly, was still there. "I thought you were leaving," she said, raising an eyebrow.

"It's an open audition," he pointed out, his tone dry. "I've seen the signs posted around school. I can sit here if I want to. I could even try out."

"Give me a break," Maxine groaned.

"Don't think I could do it, huh?" Hal looked even more stubborn.

Just then, Mrs. Mundy called, "Maxine Smyth?"

Maxine had no more time to worry about her irritating stepbrother. She picked up her copy of the play and hurried to the front of the auditorium. Trying not to let her knees tremble, she climbed the steps to the stage.

Standing all by herself in front of the drama teacher, Maxine's heart pounded. She took a deep breath, feeling the stares of the other kids who were scattered about the auditorium as she fought to control her expression. *Easy does it*, she told herself. *Don't blow your cool.*

## STEALING THE SCENE

"And you're reading . . ." The teacher looked at the list.

"Titania, if that's all right," Maxine said. She had to take another deep breath to steady herself.

"Take a copy—oh, you have one." Mrs. Mundy nodded. "All right, start in act two, scene one, with Titania's entrance. I need a boy to read the Fairy King's part. Who hasn't read yet?"

She looked around the room, but most of the boys had taken their turn.

To Maxine's horror, she saw Hal raising his hand in the back row.

"What's your name?" Mrs. Mundy asked, motioning him forward. "You didn't sign the list." She handed him a copy of the play.

"Hal Smith." Hal's expression was a comic mixture of apprehension and desperate courage.

"Fine, you may begin."

Maxine, furious at having to read against her smart-alec stepbrother, decided to put all of her nervous energy into the lines.

"What, jealous Oberon!" she began.

Hal, who had obviously never read the play, stumbled over his lines. The students watching them laughed, and Maxine blushed. If Hal ruined her chance, she'd kill him!

But Mrs. Mundy looked thoughtful. "Turn to act three, scene two. Hal, read Bottom's part. Maxine, go on with Titania."

Maxine flipped through the play until she found the right page, then directed Hal to the proper scene. She was too angry to feel any sympathy when he threw her an anguished glance, as if he'd stumbled into more than he had bargained for.

They read again, and again Hal drew laughter from the students around them. But this time Maxine realized that it wasn't just Hal's stumbling or his stage fright that evoked laughter. He sounded genuinely bewildered, just as the part called for. Did Hal have another talent she hadn't suspected?

"You can sit down, Hal," Mrs. Mundy said. "Maxine, I'd like you to read another part. John," she called to a short, stocky boy who'd already read. "Come and read opposite Maxine."

Hal went back to his seat, obviously relieved.

Maxine, still on stage, felt a stab of panic. She hadn't rehearsed this role! But you never argued with the director—at least, not during tryouts.

John walked up to the stage, holding a copy of the script. Mrs. Mundy told them which lines to read.

Maxine turned to the right scene, fighting to retain her composure.

"Why now, my love?" John read. "Why is your cheek so pale?"

Maxine smiled at him, trying to reveal all the loving devotion the part of Hermia demanded. "Be like for want of—"

A sudden crash from the front of the auditorium made them both jump, and Maxine dropped her script.

Everyone looked around, and Mrs. Mundy frowned. "Quiet, please!" she called.

Maxine located the source of the disturbance. Either Tina or Georgette had knocked a heavy three-ring binder onto the floor. But had it been an accident? Maxine bit her lip as she stooped to pick up her copy of the play. Did the two girls really think they could fluster Maxine and destroy her chance for a part?

They were in for a surprise—they wouldn't push her out of the competition so easily!

She began to read her lines again, pushing everything out of her mind except the emotion that the scene required.

At last Mrs. Mundy nodded for them to step down. Maxine was almost afraid to hope for a part.

She walked slowly down the steps, her stomach churning with nervousness. Sinking into the nearest seat before her lack of composure became obvious to the whole auditorium, Maxine swallowed hard. Had she done a good job, good enough to win a role? She would have done a lot better if Hal hadn't shown up at the last minute!

After the last student had read, Mrs. Mundy stood up and turned to look at the crowd of students. "Thank you all for coming. I'll have the cast list posted on the door tomorrow morning."

Maxine took a deep breath, trying not to look as anxious as she felt. She started out of the auditorium and found Hal waiting for her at the door.

"I hope I didn't ruin your chances," he told her.

"A little late to think of that, wouldn't you

say?" Maxine snapped. Her pent-up anger, not just at him but also at Tina and Georgette, sharpened her tone.

Hal looked embarrassed. "I didn't really intend to try out, but you made me lose my temper, trying to get rid of me like that."

"So it's my fault?"

"You could give me a chance," Hal said stubbornly. "Just because I goofed once—"

But Maxine wasn't ready to forgive him, not yet. "I'm sure you'll find new ways to do that," she said. "You seem to have so many unexpected talents."

Hal blushed. "Right," he mumbled. "Anyhow, I hope you get a part."

"We'll see," Maxine said, her voice cool.

# Chapter Five

Maxine could hardly wait to get to school the next morning. She hurried through the big front doors, heading down the hall toward the drama room. When she turned the last corner, Maxine could see a large crowd of students jostling each other as they tried to read the cast list posted on the door at the end of the hall.

Bracing herself for rejection, Maxine walked closer. She was gripping her notebooks so tightly that her fingers hurt.

"I wish I were taller," Maxine muttered as she stood in back of the group and tried to see over the heads of several students.

She recognized Georgette and Tina in front of her. They were examining the list from top to bottom, and when they turned away, both looked disappointed. Then Georgette's glance met Maxine's, and the tall girl's look of disappointment changed suddenly to one of anger.

*Why on earth would she be mad at me?* Maxine wondered. The two girls walked past without speaking, but Maxine barely noticed them as she finally edged close enough to read the list posted on the door.

She scanned the bottom of the list first for the less important roles. Tina's name was on the list of fairies, and Georgette had received the role of Hippolyta, Queen of the Amazons. The title sounded important, but Maxine knew it was a pretty small part. Georgette had probably been counting on something bigger, but that still didn't explain the furious look she had directed at Maxine.

Maxine scanned the list with her finger. Titania—Christine Nelson. Rats! Had Maxine done so badly that the drama teacher had decided not to cast her in any part?

Disappointment almost overwhelmed her, but Maxine kept reading. Not until she reached the top of the list did she see her own name: Hermia—Maxine Smyth.

Maxine gasped. Hermia was one of the leading roles!

She felt someone pound her on the back. "Congratulations!"

Maxine turned around. Standing behind her was the short, stocky boy with curly hair whom she'd read with yesterday. She glanced back at the list—*John Bates*. He was playing one of her lovers in the play. He wasn't exactly tall, dark and handsome, but she had a good part to play, and who cared? This was Shakespeare, not Tennessee Williams. They wouldn't have any passionate encounters on stage.

"Looks like we made it," he told her. "Are you excited?"

"That's putting it mildly," Maxine said. "I can't wait to start rehearsals."

"Well, I can guarantee that you won't have to wait long." John grinned. "We start this afternoon. Looks like it's going to be a family affair for you."

"What?" Maxine looked back at the posted list. She saw a familiar name that she'd somehow overlooked on her first reading. Bottom—Hal Smith. Maxine blinked, trying not to show how astonished she was. Hal had actually gotten a part!

"He's your brother, right?" John asked. "So how come his last name is spelled differently than yours?"

"Because he's my stepbrother," Maxine explained, wondering if one stage would be big enough for her and Hal.

The shrill sound of the bell made her jump. "Got to run," she told John. "See you this afternoon."

"Okay, don't be late!" he called to her as she hurried down the hall to English class.

Fortunately, Sarah and Nicole had saved her a seat. Maxine said hello, put her books down on top of the desk and looked around for Hal. She saw him standing at the back of the room, talking to a friend of his. She walked back to speak to him.

Hal looked up when she approached. "Hi. Did you get the part you wanted?"

"Actually, I got a different one—a better one!" she answered.

"Whew," Hal looked relieved. "I'm glad I didn't mess you up yesterday. I don't know why I thought of trying out for that play. It just seemed like the thing to do at the time."

Maxine stared at him. "You haven't been down to look at Mrs. Mundy's list, have you?"

Hal shook his head, his brown hair slightly disheveled, as usual. "I figured if you threw a book at me in class, I'd know you didn't get a part. I didn't want to be there when you read the list."

"Hal," Maxine giggled. "You forgot something—you tried out, too. Don't you want to know if *your* name was on the list?"

"My name?" He looked at Maxine as if she'd lost her mind. "Oh, that was just—I couldn't possibly—" He hesitated as his friend burst into laughter.

"Wait—don't tell me," the boy gasped in between laughs. "Hal Smith is going to play the female lead!"

"No, not quite. But you did get a part, Hal," Maxine said.

"You're kidding, right?" Hal's expression was far from elated. In fact, he looked horrified at the thought.

"Nope," Maxine said. "Serves you right. You're stuck with it. Rehearsals start today after school."

"No way," Hal argued. "I'll go to Mrs. Mundy

and tell her I changed my mind, I'm leaving the country, I've developed a sudden attack of mono —anything to get out of this play!"

Maxine grinned. The teacher was calling the class to order, so she had to turn back toward her desk. "See you at rehearsal," she called over her shoulder, still giggling at his expression.

"I heard you got a part in the play," Nicole said as Maxine took her seat. "That's great."

Maxine nodded. "I didn't expect to get such an important role," she confided to the other girl.

"Ladies," Mr. Ross said sternly from the front of the room. "Do you think you could focus your attention on American literature for just a *few* minutes?"

Maxine hastily opened her book, casting a quick sidelong glance at Nicole.

When the last bell rang, Maxine hurried to put her books into her locker, then headed straight for the drama room. She found the rest of the cast already assembling in the large room.

Anne, the tall, blond girl who had given such a good reading, was going to play Helena, the other female lead. A tall, dark-haired boy named Tim was the other male lead, along with John Bates. And Jake, the red-haired boy in Drama Two, had been cast as Puck, the troublemaker with the magic love potion.

Maxine took a seat toward the front of the room. Mrs. Mundy handed out copies of the play and counted her cast at the same time. "Is everyone here? I'm missing one—ah, there's our late arrival."

Maxine looked back to see Hal standing in the doorway, as if he couldn't decide whether or not he should stay.

"Come in," Mrs. Mundy urged him. "We're just getting started. But in the future, remember, promptness to rehearsals is essential."

Hal quickly sat down at an empty desk next to Maxine.

"I thought you were going to turn down the part." Maxine whispered.

"I am, as soon as I can talk to the teacher alone," Hal answered.

"*A Midsummer Night's Dream* is a comedy and a love story," Mrs. Mundy began. "We have a duke about to be married, a group of workmen planning a play in honor of the occasion, two pairs of lovers who can't get themselves sorted out, and a fairy king and queen who are quarreling and are about to confuse everyone even more with a magic love potion."

Hal sat forward in his chair, wrinkling his brow as though he was desperately trying to follow the story.

"Hermia's father wants her to marry Demetrius," the teacher continued. "However, Hermia wants to marry Lysander. Helena is in love with Demetrius, who scorns her. But when Puck, at the fairy king's command, starts handing out his love potion to the wrong people, both the young men end up in love with Helena, and

## STEALING THE SCENE 53

the fairy queen falls in love with Bottom, one of the workmen. By the end of the play, everything gets straightened out, of course."

"I should hope so," Hal muttered. "How could anyone keep up with that?"

Maxine, concentrating on the teacher, didn't listen to the rest of Hal's comical remarks. She wanted to hear all about her part and Mrs. Mundy's plans for directing the play. But later, when the cast took a short break, she noticed a very pretty girl walk up to Hal.

"Hi," she said. "I'm Christine Nelson. I'm playing Titania. We'll have several scenes together."

Hal didn't say anything at first. He just stared at Christine. Then a shy sounding "Uh, hi," found its way out of his mouth.

"I just wanted to say I'm looking forward to working with you," Christine said. She sounded slightly uncomfortable. When she pushed her soft brown hair back from her face, she revealed nice features and beautiful brown eyes.

Christine looked flustered by Hal's failure to respond. "I guess you don't want to talk about the play right now," she stammered. "Sorry I interrupted."

"Oh, no, I mean, yes, sure," Hal said quickly. "Sit down, why don't you? Let's discuss the scenes. I'm going to need a lot of help. I've never been in a play before—well, not since I was in the first grade, anyway."

"Really? But you were such a natural at the

auditions," Christine said. She pulled up a desk and sat down, and the two of them started going over the script together.

Maxine grinned. What had happened to Hal's resolve to quit?

Later, as they took a city bus home Maxine asked, "Hal, are you going to be in this play, or aren't you? I thought you were going to drop out."

"Are you kidding?" he said. "Did you ever see such a totally awesome girl? And I get to act in a love scene with *her*? I couldn't pass up an opportunity like that."

Maxine felt a flicker of surprise; Hal sounded perfectly serious. He was really taken with Christine.

"Good luck, then," Maxine told him. "I don't want to burst your bubble, but I will warn you—"

"What is it?" Hal demanded.

"You have to play the love scene wearing a donkey's head," she told him.

"What?" Hal practically yelled.

"It's true. Puck plays a magic trick on you." Maxine couldn't help giggling at the image of Hal in his future costume. "I think you'd better read the play," she said.

Hal shook his head. "Shakespeare, how could you do this to me?"

At the next stop, they got off the bus and walked the two blocks to their house in silence.

## STEALING THE SCENE

When they opened the front door, Hal called out, "Hello! Anybody home?" Nobody answered.

"I wonder where everyone is," Hal mused. "I'm going to get a snack. I'm starving."

Maxine decided to have a glass of iced tea, so she joined him in the kitchen. "Promise me you won't try any magic tricks during rehearsals," she said. "I don't want anything to go wrong with my first play in a new high school."

"Who, me?" Hal pretended to look insulted. He took a jar of peanut butter out of the cabinet overhead and began to spread it on two pieces of bread.

Maxine had her back to the doorway, but she heard Stephanie's voice. "About time you got home. B.J.'s in the garage lifting weights—building up his upper-body strength, he says. And Dad and Eve are still at the marina. I was beginning to feel like the Lone Ranger, minus Tonto."

Hal swallowed a bite of his sandwich before replying. "We've been at rehearsal. In fact, we'll be rehearsing every day after school, so we're going to be late a lot."

"Rehearsal?" Stephanie queried. "I knew Maxine was trying out for the play, but what were you doing there?"

"Believe it or not, I've got a part in the play, too," Hal told his sister. "I'm an actor!"

"Hollywood, look out." Stephanie threw up her hands. "You mean both of you are star struck now?"

"Hey, Steph, you know what? You could work on the play, too. Mrs. Mundy said she'll need people for the stage crew," Hal suggested.

"Why would I want to do that?" Stephanie demanded. "I have plenty of things to do."

*Sure*, Maxine thought. *Like sulk some more in your bedroom.* She stared at her stepsister. Wasn't Stephanie ever going to grow up?

"It was just an idea," Hal said, shrugging. "Take it or leave it."

# Chapter Six

On Friday afternoon Stephanie stepped off the school bus and walked slowly up to the house. As usual, Hal and Maxine had stayed after school.

"Rehearsal again," Stephanie said to herself. "That's all they do. What a pain."

But, as she unlocked the front door Stephanie hesitated a moment before walking into the quiet house.

"Hurry up," B.J. said, suddenly coming up behind her. He looked as if he had run home from school instead of taking the bus. "I want a snack, then I've got iron to pump."

"Pardon me," Stephanie said with exaggerated courtesy, stepping inside to let the younger boy hurry through the doorway.

"Mom?" B.J. called, but there was no answer. "She must be at the marina again," he grumbled.

Stephanie was too discouraged to be hungry. She left B.J. in the kitchen and went on to her bedroom. Dropping her books onto her desk, Stephanie threw herself atop the rumpled bed.

She felt so lonely and left out. Everyone had something to do except her. Maxine was busy with her play, and even Hal had allowed himself to be roped into acting. B.J. spent all his time lifting weights or throwing his stupid baseball. Her dad was always busy at the marina, and Eve worked in the marina office.

"I feel so useless," Stephanie muttered to herself.

She considered pulling her journal out from its hiding place under her mattress, but even that didn't appeal to her. She got up and went back to the kitchen.

If she hadn't known better, she would have sworn a hungry army had marched through the room instead of one starving teenager. B.J. had carved a large chunk out of a ham, then left the rest of the ham on the counter, along with an open loaf of bread and a jar of mustard. Shaking her head, Stephanie took the knife and sliced a small piece to chew on while she dialed Carol's number.

The phone rang twice, then, to Stephanie's relief, someone answered.

"Carol? Thank goodness. If you hadn't been at home, I would have screamed!"

"I got out of volleyball practice early. What's up?"

"Nothing; that's the problem," Stephanie told her best friend. "I'm so *bored*."

"You probably just need something to do after school," Carol suggested. "Aren't you working on the school newspaper this year?"

"I don't know," Stephanie said. "I've thought about it, but the staff isn't organized yet. I'm not sure if—"

"Just a minute!" Carol yelled to someone in the background, cutting Stephanie off midsentence. "I'll call you back in a sec, Stephanie. My mother says if I don't pick up my room right now, I'll lose phone privileges for the weekend."

"Okay." Stephanie sighed and hung up the receiver. She looked at the cluttered counter and briefly considered cleaning it up. But B.J. was the one who had made the mess; let him put the stuff away, or get into trouble with Eve if he didn't. The thought made Stephanie grin.

She hacked another small piece of meat off the ham—it was tender and very good—while she waited for the phone to ring again. When it did, she grabbed the receiver and held it to her ear.

"That was fast," she said.

There was a slight pause on the other end. "Hello? Is this the Smith residence?"

It was a boy's voice, not Carol's. "Uh, yes," Stephanie answered slowly.

"Is Maxine there?"

Stephanie frowned. *I should have known it wouldn't be for me*, she told herself crossly. "She's at a play rehearsal. Can I give her a message?"

"Oh, hi, Stephanie. This is Kevin Fowler. Just tell Maxine I called. On second thought, I think I'll run over to the school. She might like a ride home."

"Right," Stephanie said. It took all her willpower not to slam the phone back into its cradle. Kevin was obviously totally overwhelmed by Miss Perfect. But did he ever give Stephanie a second look? No! How could life be so unfair?

The phone rang again almost at once, but this time Stephanie let it ring several times before she picked it up.

"Hello?"

"It's me," Carol said. "Were you expecting Prince Charming?"

"If he called, he'd ask to speak to Maxine," Stephanie said bitterly. "I can't believe it, Carol. Kevin Fowler is crazy about my dumb stepsister."

"You can't blame him, Stephanie," Carol said. "She's really pretty, and she always looks terrific—I mean, her hair, her clothes—"

"Thanks a lot," Stephanie snapped. "Are you saying I'm so plain no boy would look at me?" Stephanie bit her lip, sure that she would burst into tears if her friend agreed with her.

"Of course not," Carol said. "But sometimes I wonder if you're doing it on purpose."

"Doing what?" Stephanie frowned at the telephone. "Stop talking in riddles."

"Well, you refuse to use any makeup, and your clothes—"

"Not you, too!" Stephanie flared. "You used to wear jeans every day, just like me, you know. You never worried about lipstick and mascara and all that other stuff."

"*Used to*," Carol pointed out. "We both did that, when we were younger. We're not ten years old anymore, Stephanie. Sometimes I think you've stepped into a time warp, like some science-fiction character. Since your mother died, it's like you're just spinning your wheels, refusing to go forward."

"That's not true," Stephanie yelled. "Some friend you are!" Without waiting for an answer, she banged the phone down.

This was too much. If even Carol, her own best friend, started criticizing her, who did she have left? Stephanie hurried to her room and slammed the door behind her.

She pulled out her journal and opened to an empty page.

"Dear Mom," she wrote. "Nobody likes me today. I wish you were still here."

Through tears, her writing blurred. Swallowing hard, Stephanie continued to write. "Why am I never good enough for anybody? Nobody likes me the way I am, and I'm not going to change!"

Sometime later she heard Hal's voice, and later still, the sound of a car in the driveway. Was her father home at last? Stephanie got up from her bed and went to look out the front window, but instead of her father, she saw Kevin and Maxine leaning on the hood of Kevin's car, deep in conversation. Kevin had his arm around Maxine's shoulder. As she watched, they both laughed at some remark she couldn't hear.

"I hope they choke," Stephanie whispered to herself.

When Maxine came into the house, she smiled

at Stephanie, who was still standing in the hallway.

"Glad it's Friday?" Maxine asked.

"Sure," Stephanie answered. Without stopping to stare at Maxine's surprised face, she hurried past her and out the front door. But Kevin had already pulled out of the driveway.

*He didn't even say hello to me*, Stephanie thought miserably.

She heard the sound of another car, and her father's blue sedan drove up. But after Eve got out, Don Smith pulled back into the street. Stephanie's stepmother walked up the driveway toward her.

"Hello." Eve smiled at her. "How was school?"

"All right, I guess. Where's Dad off to?" Stephanie asked, trying to look as if nothing had upset her. She followed Eve into the house.

"Don's going to put gas in the car. He'll be right back. I asked him to drop me off first so I could get dinner started. I didn't mean to be so late getting home," Eve said, glancing at her watch. "Fortunately, I've got some fresh vegetables and a nice ham for dinner, so it won't take long—oh, dear."

Stephanie stared past Eve's shoulder and saw the platter that had held the ham, still sitting on the kitchen counter. All that remained now was a large hambone, with a few pieces of meat clinging to it.

"Good heavens," Eve said faintly. "What happened to my ham?"

Hal, coming in through the garage with B.J. behind him, heard the question. He looked slightly guilty. "I had a little to snack on after school," he admitted. "I was starving."

"A little?" Eve repeated. "You ate the whole ham!"

"I had some, too," B.J. said. "It was a long day at school, Mom, and the lunch today was terrible. Chili and beans, ugh."

Stephanie said, "I only had a little piece."

Eve shook her head. "Well, I hope you all enjoyed it, because that was our dinner. Now what am I going to cook?"

The two boys looked at each other and, apparently deciding that this was no time to linger at the scene of the crime, they ducked into the hallway.

Stephanie followed them, in no mood to volunteer her help. Eve was the master chef; let *her* figure out a new menu.

Stephanie didn't return to the kitchen until she heard her father come into the house half an hour later. By that time, an appetizing aroma had begun to drift through the house, so she figured Eve must have come up with something to eat.

"Smells good," Don said. "Dinner almost ready?"

"If you could call it that," Eve answered cryptically.

Stephanie heard the exchange as she began to set the table. She wondered what Eve had found for dinner. Something in a big pot bubbled on the stovetop. On the other side of the kitchen,

Maxine was busy tossing a salad, and soon the two boys reappeared. They all sat down around the kitchen table.

Eve brought a large tureen of soup to the table. "Homemade vegetable soup," she told them. "Flavored with hambone."

Hal and B.J. looked at each other, then quickly down at the table. Maxine, who hadn't witnessed the earlier ham fiasco, said, "It looks good."

They all took steaming bowls of the soup and helpings of salad. It didn't take long to empty the soup tureen.

"Great," B.J. said. "What's the next course?"

Eve met his inquiring gaze with a slightly forced smile. "That's it, I'm afraid."

"That's all?" Don looked a little surprised. "I thought you went to the supermarket yesterday."

"I did," Eve agreed. "It's going to take me a while to learn how to shop for our family."

"If you had warned me you needed groceries, I would have stopped by the store on the way home," Don said.

"If I'd known the cupboard was bare, I would have," Eve answered, beginning to sound irritated.

Don frowned. "I can't read minds."

"Neither can I," Eve said. Her smile had faded.

B.J. looked uncomfortable. "I'm not hungry anymore," he said. "I've got some homework to do." He slipped out of his chair and left the kitchen.

"I need to feed the rabbits," Hal murmured,

obviously embarrassed. He headed for the backyard.

The two adults continued to argue. "You should keep a grocery list," Don said.

"I do *not* need any advice on running my kitchen," Eve snapped.

Maxine, her lips set in a forced smile, said, "I've got homework, too," and left the room.

Stephanie hurried after her, anxious to get away from the fight in the kitchen. She followed the older girl down the hall to her room, in time to hear B.J., who had waited for his sister, ask quietly, "Do you think they'll get a divorce, too?"

Maxine shook her head, but Stephanie saw that her face was pale.

Stephanie went into her room and left the other two in the hallway.

A divorce? Then Maxine would leave, and Stephanie wouldn't have to worry about having a stepsister who was the most popular girl at Bayview High.

Somehow the thought didn't lift her spirits. Even then, would Kevin Fowler ever give plain old Stephanie a second look?

"I doubt it," Stephanie groaned, thumping her pillow. "Why are boys so dumb?"

# Chapter Seven

"Hurry up!" Stephanie yelled, pounding on the bathroom door Saturday morning. "You're not the only person who wants a shower, you know."

Maxine, who had just stepped out of the shower herself, made a face. "In a minute," she called back as she hung up her towel, refusing to be rushed. She hadn't been able to sleep because she had been worrying so much about the quarrel Don and her mother had had the night before. Staring into the mirror at the dark circles under her eyes, Maxine shook her head. She couldn't face Kevin looking like a corpse, especially on their first real date. She still felt a bit nervous about going out on a small boat, but for someone as nice and as handsome as Kevin, it was worth a try. Opening her make up case, she set to work.

When she finally opened the door and stepped into the hall, Stephanie was obviously fuming. "About time," she snapped, and hurried into the bathroom before one of the boys appeared.

Maxine walked down the hall and into the kitchen. A large note was propped on the counter. We're at the marina, her mother had written. Fresh blueberry muffins on top of the stove. Then, a postscript at the bottom, in large letters, NO MORE THAN THREE EACH, PLEASE!"

Maxine grinned. Mom was learning. And if her mother and Don were working together at the marina today, they must have made up.

Maxine put the kettle on to boil and made herself a mug of tea. She drank her tea and ate two delicious muffins while she glanced over the morning paper. When Stephanie walked into the kitchen, she read the note without comment, but she put three muffins on a plate and began to eat them.

The sound of a car in the driveway made Maxine jump up and look out the window. "There's Kevin," she told Stephanie. "Tell him I'll be right there, would you? I've got to brush my teeth."

Stephanie shot her a withering glance as she ran for the bathroom. *Someone* had obviously gotten up on the wrong side of the bed this morning, Maxine thought. As usual.

When she returned, Kevin was standing in the hallway.

"I've put a new coat of paint on her," he was telling Stephanie. "I like to keep the *Windsong* spotless. Haven't seen you at the marina lately. Busy with school?"

Stephanie muttered an answer, but Kevin had turned toward Maxine. "Ready to go?" he asked.

"All set." Maxine smiled at him. "See you later, Stephanie."

Kevin held the front door open for her.

"Beautiful day," Maxine said as she stepped through the doorway. She looked up at the blue sky; fluffy white clouds slid along, pushed by a strong breeze.

"Perfect for sailing," Kevin told her. "You're going to love it."

Maxine wasn't so sure, but she smiled and didn't answer.

When they reached the marina, Kevin parked his small car. They waved at Don, talking to a boat owner at one end of the marina, then walked out to the spot where Kevin's sailboat waited. Maxine, watching the small boat bob and shift on the water, felt a moment of apprehension. Was this going to be as easy as she'd expected?

But, after all, how hard could sailing be? It was only a little boat, she told herself, not a great big one. And they probably wouldn't go very far out in the bay. But just watching the shifting water made her a little dizzy, and she looked away.

"Jump in," Kevin told her. "I'll take care of the lines."

Maxine saw that sturdy-looking ropes, tied securely around posts on the dockside, tethered the boat to the dock. Holding her breath, she jumped across the small stretch of water, landing easily on the deck of the boat. She was glad she had worn her new sneakers.

"Here." Kevin tossed her an orange life jacket. "Just to be safe."

Maxine frowned at the unflattering color, but she thrust her arms through the vest and fixed the straps. Then she looked around for a place to sit. Maxine was startled to see a long pole swing around the front of the boat, parallel to the deck. She ducked just in time.

"What was that?"

"The boom," Kevin explained, still busy adjusting the sails. "The mainsail is the big one, here, and the other, smaller sail is called the jib. The *Windsong* is a small sloop."

"Right," Maxine agreed. Hal had said something about sloops the last time she'd come to the marina.

"Here's the wheel," Kevin continued. "It turns the rudder and steers the boat. These lines," he said, pointing to several thick ropes tied near the big metal wheel, "trim the mainsail."

"Okay . . . I guess," Maxine said.

Kevin grinned. "You'll get the hang of it soon," he promised.

"I wouldn't bet on that," Maxine muttered.

When they moved away from the dock, the little boat rocked and shifted with the waves. Grabbing the side of the boat, Maxine gulped. She didn't know that a small boat could tilt so much! Her stomach rolled unpleasantly, and she had to swallow hard.

The wind, which had felt so pleasant on the dock, now blew mercilessly. Her carefully arranged hair flew into her face, becoming hopelessly tangled. A sudden high wave hit the side of the boat, and its spray slapped her face. Maxine gasped and wiped her eyes, which stung from the saltwater. *Great, now I probably have mascara streaked all over my cheeks.*

She felt damp and cold. Her thin navy blue top, which had seemed fine for a warm day, now clung to her, and even her slacks felt damp and clammy. Maxine shivered inside her life jacket, her bare arms covered with goose bumps.

"Isn't this great?" Kevin yelled over the wind.

"Great," Maxine muttered, trying to force her chattering lips into a smile.

"Hang on to the side," Kevin called. "I'm going to show you how we tack to windward."

As far as Maxine could tell, this meant jumping around madly while the boat careened first to one side, then to another. Her stomach rolled along with the boat.

"You see," Kevin explained, "it's the only way to move against the direction of the wind."

"Why would you want to?" Maxine asked. "It isn't worth it."

But the flapping sails and the shrieking of several sea gulls overhead drowned out her words.

*I'm going to be sick,* Maxine thought. *And I'll die of embarrassment, if my stomach doesn't kill me first.*

Her stomach lurched, and she turned toward the side of the boat. But her feet landed on a wet spot on the deck, and then flew out from under her. She hit the deck with a solid thump.

"You okay?" Kevin yelled.

Maxine lay back against the shifting deck.

"Can we turn this thing around?" she yelled. Taking a deep breath, she attempted to scramble back to her feet.

"What?" He looked at her, confused. "Mind the boom."

Maxine ducked for the tenth time, and felt her head spin. "I don't feel so good, Kevin."

"What?" Kevin repeated, his attention on the sail as it fluttered in the wind.

"I'm *seasick*!" Maxine shrieked. "I want to go home!"

Later, when she finally felt the wood planking of the marina firmly beneath her feet, Maxine thought grimly that some things were just not what they were cracked up to be. Sailboats, for example. Even blond-haired, blue-eyed sailors had lost some of their appeal. No matter how cute Kevin was, he wasn't worth this kind of agony, ever again.

"I'm sorry," she told Kevin, trying to salvage their date. "I could have taken some motion-sickness pills, but I didn't think I would get seasick. I'm sorry I cut your sailing short."

"That's okay," Kevin assured her. "I'm sorry you don't feel well. Would you like to do something else?"

Maxine, who still felt her stomach heave every time she glanced at the shifting water, shook her head. "I think I'd better go home," she said. "I just want to lie down for a while."

"Sure," Kevin said. He took her arm and they walked slowly out to his parked car.

When they reached the Smith home, Kevin walked around the car and opened the door for Maxine.

"Are you okay?" he asked, sounding anxious. "You're still so pale."

Maxine nodded, then wished she hadn't. Her head still wanted to spin, and her stomach was unsteady. "I just want to lie down. Sorry I turned out to be such a party pooper."

"It's not your fault," Kevin assured her. "Can I call you tomorrow?"

"Sure," Maxine said. "Thanks for the sailing lesson. It was definitely a new experience." She grinned a bit wryly at him.

He walked her to the front door, then Maxine said good-bye and hurried inside toward her room.

Stephanie stuck her head out of her bedroom, apparently curious about who was home.

"What are you doing home already?" she demanded. "I mean, you and Kevin didn't have an argument, did you?" She sounded almost hopeful.

Maxine shook her head. "*Mal de mer*," she said succinctly. "I wasn't meant to be a sailor."

"What?" Stephanie frowned, and her voice quivered with emotion. "You're lucky enough to go sailing with Kevin Fowler, and you get seasick? Talk about a waste. Now I've heard everything!"

Maxine blinked in surprise, but she didn't have the energy to argue with her stepsister. "You can yell if you want," she said. "I'm going to lie down." She shut the door of her bedroom and collapsed onto the bed. Thank goodness for a surface that didn't tilt!

Why was Stephanie acting so weird? Was it because of Kevin? Maxine didn't even have enough energy to pursue that thought. Willing her head to stop spinning, Maxine drifted off to sleep.

When she woke, the slant of the sunlight had altered, and she realized that it was afternoon. Maxine lifted her head cautiously, pleased to find that the room remained steady. Her stomach had calmed, too. Relieved, Maxine stretched her arms and legs cautiously. Her muscles were sore from leapfrogging around the boat, not to mention the one time she'd fallen right on her rear end. And all she'd done was almost tip the little boat over! Maxine grinned at the memory. If Kevin didn't call tomorrow, she couldn't really blame him. As first dates went, today had really bombed.

Then she remembered Stephanie's strange behavior. Maxine lay back against her pillow and tried to sort out her stepsister's unreasonable tantrums. It was true that Stephanie had never been the most cheerful member of their newly blended family, but this week had been worse than most. Every time she had seen Maxine, Stephanie seemed like she wanted to bite her head off.

Come to think of it, every time Kevin appeared, Stephanie turned into a major grouch. Maxine remembered the expression on Stephanie's face when she and Kevin left for the marina, and Stephanie's comment when Maxine returned from the sailing trip. "What a waste!"

Did Stephanie have a crush on Kevin?

Surely not. Kevin had mentioned Stephanie only casually. He obviously had no romantic interest in the younger girl.

But, Maxine admitted to herself, that didn't mean that Stephanie's feelings were the same as Kevin's. After all, Kevin was very good-looking, with his blond hair, deep blue eyes, and tanned skin. And he was so pleasant and always smiling, that he was easy to like.

If Stephanie had a secret crush on Kevin, was it worth risking a continuing war at home to go on dating him?

Maybe it wouldn't even come to that, Maxine told herself. Maybe Kevin would decide that he and Maxine had different interests. She was busy with the play, and he had his sailboat. And even fortified with motion sickness pills, Maxine shuddered at the thought of another excursion on the water.

"I'm definitely a landlubber," she said aloud. "But I think I'm going to live, because I feel hungry."

A cup of tea and some crackers sounded wonderful. Maxine dragged herself out of bed. When she entered the hallway, Maxine heard the phone

## STEALING THE SCENE 75

ring once. The second ring was cut off as someone picked up the receiver.

Coming into the kitchen, Maxine saw that Stephanie, frowning fiercely, had answered the phone.

"It's for you," Stephanie said. "As usual!" She dropped the phone on the counter, heedless of the clatter it made, then stomped out of the kitchen.

Maxine watched her go, and gingerly picked up the phone, almost in a daze from Stephanie's odd reaction. "Hello?"

"Wow," Kevin said. "What was that? Did the roof fall in?"

"Sorry," Maxine told him. "Stephanie dropped the phone." *On purpose, of course*, she thought, but didn't say it out loud.

"Are you feeling better?" He asked, sounding genuinely concerned.

Maxine felt her resolve to stop seeing Kevin weaken. If he weren't such a nice guy, it would be a lot easier to end their budding relationship. "Yes, I am, thanks," she answered. "I took a nap, and it helped."

"Good," he told her. "There's a football game tonight at school. Would you like to go with me?"

Maxine hesitated. What about Stephanie? A football game with Kevin would be fun, but was it worth Stephanie's antagonism? And if she and Stephanie continued to feud, what would it do to Eve and Don's marriage?

"I don't think so, Kevin."

"If you don't feel up to it, I understand," he said quickly. "There's another game next week."

"It's not that," Maxine forced herself to say.

The phone line was silent for a moment, then Kevin said, "I thought you liked me."

"I do," Maxine said, moved by the hurt in his voice. "I'm just not sure we have enough in common. I mean, you like to sail, and boats make me turn green. And I'm so busy rehearsing for the play—I just don't think I'll have much time to go out for a while, Kevin."

"Tell you what. We'll talk about it next week," Kevin said.

"But—," Maxine began.

"I don't give up easily," he told her. "See you at school."

As she hung up the phone, Maxine sighed. If she had to be honest with herself, not getting involved with Kevin didn't have a lot to do with different interests, or the problem with Stephanie. If she became too attached to this place, to the people here, it would be that much harder to leave if her mother's new marriage didn't work out. Her throat ached as she remembered all the friends she'd left behind when they moved from Washington, D.C.

Divorce meant so many good-byes.

And if one marriage could fail, who could say whether the next one would last?

She wasn't sure how much she liked Kevin, and she wasn't sure she wanted to find out. The more she liked him—really liked him—the harder it would be to break up.

What was the use of liking somebody if you only got hurt? Sometimes it was better to be safe than sorry. Wasn't it?

# Chapter Eight

Stephanie watched Maxine and Kevin pull out of the driveway Saturday morning and gritted her teeth. She would have crawled across broken glass to go sailing with Kevin Fowler, but did he ever think to ask her? No, she was just the kid hanging around the marina. He treated her like a little sister; talk about insulting!

Stephanie put her empty glass in the dishwasher and wandered back into the living room. The day stretched ahead of her, empty and boring. She'd meant to go to the beach with Carol, but after her friend's comments yesterday, they'd never completed their plans. Stephanie thought of calling Carol and apologizing, but she was still too angry. Everyone in the world seemed to want to change her.

"I'm perfectly happy the way I am," Stephanie told herself. Then, realizing the irony of the statement—she'd seldom felt less happy than she did right now—she grinned reluctantly at herself. Flipping on the TV, she tried to lose herself in the latest rock-music videos.

When Maxine came home early from her sailing date, Stephanie felt even more disgusted. Kevin was the nicest boy at school, and Maxine didn't even appreciate him.

A few minutes later, Stephanie heard someone in the kitchen. She went to the doorway and saw Hal holding open the refrigerator door, peering inside.

"What are you doing home?"

"Dad sent me home to pick up some papers he forgot. I thought I'd grab a bite to eat while I'm here."

"Out of hot dogs at the marina?"

"No, but I'm broke, and Gator's cut off my credit at the hot-dog stand." Hal made a face. "Bummer."

"Did I hear someone mention food?" B.J. appeared in the doorway, his baseball glove in one hand.

"Say the magic word," Hal joked.

The two boys rummaged through the meat tray, making themselves mammoth sandwiches.

Stephanie speared a pickle for herself, and sat on one of the chairs while the two boys ate.

"Is Maxine all right?" Hal asked, between bites. "She looked pretty green."

"How'd you know? Did you see her?" Stephanie asked. "On Kevin's sailboat, I mean?"

"Only when they came back to the marina. She was as wet as a cat who's been left out in the rain, and about as cheerful."

Stephanie giggled. If that didn't discourage Kevin's attraction, what would? Feeling better, she took another pickle.

Hal finished his sandwich and stood up. "I've got to get back to the marina. Like to come with me, B.J.?"

The younger boy hesitated. "Well—"

"I promised I'd work in the bait shop this afternoon, but Dad might have time to take you out on the bay."

B.J.'s expression hardened. "Nope," he said flatly. "I have to work out with my weights."

Hal shook his head as B.J. hurried out of the kitchen. "Put my foot in that one, didn't I?"

Stephanie refused to sympathize. "Clean up your mess," she told her brother.

Hal groaned, but he began to clear off the counter.

When Hal left, Stephanie lingered in the kitchen, drinking a glass of juice and watching the vines around the kitchen window flutter in the breeze. She thought about Kevin, remembering how handsome he looked when he smiled. He had the nicest blue eyes she had ever seen. But would Kevin ever see her as more than another anonymous sophomore?

The phone rang, and Stephanie hurried to answer it. Maybe Carol had decided to forget about their quarrel. "Hello?" she said in a polite tone.

"Is Maxine there?"

## STEALING THE SCENE 81

It was Kevin again! Even seasick and grumpy, Maxine still had her claws into him. What magic powers did that girl have, anyhow?

As if on cue, a sleepy-looking Maxine appeared in the kitchen doorway.

"It's for you," Stephanie told her. "As usual!" She dropped the phone on the counter in her hurry to get out of the room. Hearing Maxine and Kevin coo at each other was more than Stephanie could bear.

Back in her own room, Stephanie pulled her journal out from its hiding place under her mattress and curled up on the bed.

"K.F. is the cutest boy I know," she wrote, "but sometimes he doesn't seem very smart! Why can't he see that Maxine is not his type—and I am?"

Stephanie stayed in her room till dinner time, when Hal pounded on her door.

"Come out, come out, wherever you are! Dinner's ready!" he sang.

She walked into the kitchen and found Eve stirring two large pots of tomato sauce. "One spaghetti sauce with onion, one without," Eve told them. "The spaghetti is ready; help yourselves."

Even Stephanie couldn't fault the large plate of spaghetti that she took to the table.

"Delicious," Don said after swallowing his first bite.

The two boys were eating just as ravenously as

if they hadn't devoured huge sandwiches at lunch.

"No garlic toast?" B.J. asked, looking around the table.

Eve shook her head. "*Someone*," she pointed out mildly, "ate all the bread in the house. Have some salad."

"Why don't we just set up our table in the middle of the supermarket?" Don suggested. "Nothing else will keep these bottomless pits filled."

He grinned as he spoke, and Eve smiled across the table at him.

Stephanie, glad to see that her father and Eve were acting normal again, reached for the pitcher of iced tea, ready to fill her glass.

"Who put lemons in the tea?" she asked, obviously displeased.

"I did," Maxine said. "What about it?"

"I like my tea without lemon," Stephanie complained.

"She's sour enough all by herself," B.J. said, grinning at his own joke.

"Very funny." Stephanie tossed her thick hair back and went to the refrigerator for a glass of fruit juice.

They ate silently for a few minutes.

Don looked at Maxine and Hal and asked, "How are the play rehearsals coming?"

"Good," Maxine told them. "I've still got a lot of lines to learn, though."

"Some of my lines are hard," Hal said. "The

rehearsals last so long, too. That reminds me—Steph, I need a favor."

"What?" Stephanie looked at her brother suspiciously. "If you want me to feed your rabbits, forget it."

"Nothing like that," he assured her. "It's about the play. We need someone to write some publicity stories, and not just for the school paper, either. We're sending them to all the area papers. And I volunteered you for the job."

"Thanks a lot." Stephanie glared at him. Help Maxine be famous in her first play? Fat chance! "Who said I have time to do PR?"

The whole table paused to stare at her. Hal turned red, but it was their father who answered. "You don't seem exactly overwhelmed with homework, Stephanie. And if you have another occupation, I haven't noticed."

Stephanie frowned. "I'll be writing for the school paper when Mr. Forrest gets the staff organized." Too late, she saw the trap yawning before her.

"Then you'll be killing two birds with one stone," Don observed. "You'll have your first story ready for the school paper, and the drama group can use it for local publicity, too."

Hal added, "I told them you'd do a good job, Steph. Come on, one article wouldn't take long. I know you're a good writer."

Stephanie couldn't think of any more excuses. "Oh, all right," she muttered.

"Good," Hal grinned at her. "You can come to

rehearsal Monday after school and collect the information you need. I'll introduce you to the cast."

Stephanie jabbed a piece of lettuce with her fork. "I can't wait."

# Chapter Nine

On Monday, Stephanie sat through her classes unable to concentrate. All she could think about was the rehearsal after school. The thought of having to write a feature story about Maxine and her big part still rankled her. Who wanted to make Maxine more popular than she was already? But Stephanie had promised Hal she'd do the story, so she didn't have much choice. At least there were plenty of other people in the play. Her own brother, for one. She could write about him.

Carol nodded stiffly when they met in the classroom; her friend was obviously still offended by Stephanie's outburst. Stephanie wanted to apologize, but some lingering hint of stubbornness held her back. When lunchtime came, though, Stephanie couldn't stand the thought of having to eat alone.

She waited for Carol in the hallway, stepping out to confront her friend when she finally walked past.

"Carol, I'm a real jerk," she announced.

Carol looked startled. "What?"

"I shouldn't have yelled at you the other day," Stephanie apologized. "I'm sorry. It's just that Maxine and Eve keep giving me hints about improving my appearance—leaving copies of *Seventeen* and *Young Miss* in my room, things like that. I feel like one of those 'before' pictures; everybody thinks I need to be improved. So when you started—"

Carol nodded. "I'm sorry, too. I'm not trying to tell you what to do, Stephanie. I just wanted to help. But if you want to look—" She paused to look over Stephanie's worn jeans and faded T-shirt. "Well, *casual*, that's your choice."

"Still friends?" Stephanie asked, her tone a little wary.

"Of course," Carol said. "Although you cost me a lazy day in the sun. I wanted to go to the beach with you last weekend, but since I didn't have a good excuse, I ended up at home baby-sitting my little brother."

"We'll go next Saturday," Stephanie promised, feeling better. "Tell your mother we've already made plans and absolutely can't change them."

"Especially for bratty little brothers," Carol agreed, grinning.

"At least you only have one brother," Stephanie told her. "I've got half a platoon living in my house."

Giggling, they headed for the cafeteria.

\* \* \*

## STEALING THE SCENE

When the final bell rang that afternoon, Stephanie put her books into her locker and headed for the auditorium. In spite of herself, she began to feel curious. What would she think of the rehearsal—was the play as absorbing as her two resident actors seemed to think? Hal and Maxine talked of little else lately besides the big production.

The stage was cluttered with long planks of wood and big rolls of canvas. Stephanie stepped cautiously around the edge of the pile, surveying the crowd until she spotted her brother in a group of cast members.

"Hi, Steph," Hal called. "Glad you came. This is my sister, Stephanie," he told the brown-haired girl standing next to him. "Steph, this is Christine Nelson. She plays Titania, the fairy queen. We have a few scenes together. She's trying to get me through this play so that I don't pull out *all* my hair."

His brown hair, as usual, seemed to be standing on end, but Christine didn't make the obvious joke. She smiled at Hal without sarcasm. "You're doing a great job, Hal. I bet you steal the whole show."

"Sure, when I fall on my face," Hal groaned.

"You're just being modest," Christine assured him. She turned to Stephanie. "Hi."

"Hello." Stephanie smiled at the other girl while she thought, *Hal? Modest?*

Christine had a particularly sweet smile. "I'm glad you could come down and help us out," she said.

Hal was staring at Christine as if she were some rare painting in a museum, Stephanie noticed. Beautiful, but too precious to touch. She tried not to giggle. Had Hal fallen in love? It was too funny!

Then she remembered that she was supposed to be collecting information for her news story. She looked around at the lumber and canvas piled on the stage.

"What's all this?" Stephanie asked the other two. She had brought her notepad, and she felt quite professional as she pulled out her pencil.

"Wood for frames, and canvas to stretch over them to make the flats," Christine explained. "For the sets. We've been building flats all week, then we paint them. I always end up with paint on me from head to foot when I do this."

Stephanie grinned. "So you've acted in plays before?"

"A couple," Christine said. "But you'd better talk to our stars, Anne and Tim and John and Maxine."

*Maxine again*, Stephanie thought, frowning. But someone else interrupted.

"Are you doing an article about the play?"

Stephanie nodded. She recognized the tall girl, Georgette something, a junior. Stephanie had seen her around school.

"I'm Georgette McDivott," the other girl said, "with two *t*'s."

Stephanie managed not to giggle as she wrote down the name. "Which role are you playing?"

"Hippolyta, Queen of the Amazons," Georgette explained, frowning just a little. "I'm betrothed to Thesus, the duke. That means engaged," she explained.

"I *know*." Stephanie said sternly.

Georgette didn't seem to notice. "I had a part in two plays last year," she told Stephanie, obviously trying to impress her. "I really expected to have a better part in this play, but—there are all these new people in drama this year. I suppose Mrs. Mundy felt she had to give them a chance."

Stephanie, seeing the way Georgette glared at Maxine, who stood in the corner talking to a curly-haired boy with broad shoulders, could guess which 'new person' Georgette was miffed at.

"What's wrong with your part?" she asked bluntly.

"Are you kidding?" Georgette answered. "I have less than thirty lines in the whole play! What chance is that to display any acting talent?" She sniffed.

Stephanie thought about the question. "Even a small part should be well acted, though, shouldn't it?"

"Well, of course," Georgette looked offended. "Whose side are you on, anyhow? Oh, I get it. You're related to Maxine, aren't you?"

Stephanie felt herself tense up. "Not exactly," she said. "She's my stepsister."

"No wonder." Georgette looked exasperated by the whole business. "I suppose you'll spend the whole article talking about Maxine."

"I will not!" Stephanie snapped. "I wouldn't

want to. I mean, that wouldn't be professional. I'll write about *all* the players."

"Then let me tell you some more about my background," Georgette said.

She babbled on for several minutes, till Stephanie finally excused herself. "I better talk to some of the other cast members." She said, slipping away. Glad to leave the gregarious Georgette behind, Stephanie headed across the stage.

"Hi, Stephanie," Maxine said as she approached. "This is John, Tim, and Anne."

The blond girl nodded, and the two boys grinned.

"Here to make us famous?" John asked her.

"Writing a publicity story," Stephanie told him. "Spell your last names for me."

She wrote them all down, and the roles they were playing. She also discovered that Anne had acted in four plays, playing the lead once; John had held leading roles in three productions, Tim in two, and Maxine, to her stepsister's surprise, in no less than six.

"Back in Washington," Maxine explained, "we had a good drama coach, and a large group of actors. My favorite play was *West Side Story*."

"Don't tell me—you played Maria?" Anne looked at Maxine with genuine respect. "I didn't know you could sing as well as act."

"A little." Maxine shrugged. "I took lessons."

Stephanie was startled. She hadn't realized that Maxine had so much stage experience. She thought of Georgette's comments, which were beginning to sound a lot like sour grapes.

## STEALING THE SCENE

She continued to take notes as the four came up with anecdotes about past performances. Then talk shifted to the current play.

"Shakespeare is hard," Tim confessed. "But once you get past the iambic pentameter—the rhythm of some of the lines—the plays are really good. Mrs. Mundy is a big help. She can always explain what we're supposed to be talking about if I get lost."

"Which only happens every other line," Anne teased.

They all laughed.

"Sounds like these rehearsals aren't all work," a boy's voice said. "What's so funny?"

Stephanie recognized the voice at once. She whirled around to stare at the new arrival.

"Kevin! What are you doing here?" Maxine asked, sounding almost as surprised as Stephanie felt.

"Mrs. Mundy said she needed people to work backstage," Kevin said, grinning. "Here I am."

"Good, we need some help," Anne told him.

"As long as I don't have to put on any make up," Kevin said. "Actually, Mrs. Mundy wants someone to move the plants between scenes, she's using a bunch of silk trees to make up the forest."

Stephanie looked down at her notepad, afraid to meet Kevin's eyes. Just standing next to him made her heart beat faster, and he hadn't even noticed that she was there. All he seemed to see was Maxine. It was clear that Kevin had acquired this sudden interest in drama for only one reason.

Maxine seemed to suspect the same thing. "What a coincidence," she said quietly, "you joining the drama group."

Kevin grinned. "Told you I didn't give up easily," he said.

Stephanie suppressed a groan of disgust. "I think I have enough information for my story," she said loudly. "Guess I'll be going."

"Why don't you hang around and watch the rehearsal," Anne offered. "You might find another twist for your story. And at least you'll get a chuckle or two, watching us goof up our lines."

"Hey, are you talking about me?" Tim objected, grinning.

"I think I'll stay," Kevin said. "Wouldn't hurt if I knew what the play's about. Come on, Stephanie. We'll go sit at the side and watch."

Stephanie felt her face flush at the casual invitation; she hoped that Kevin didn't notice her confusion. She followed him toward the side of the stage, out of everyone's way. What else could she do? And how could she pass up the chance to sit side by side, so close to Kevin? She wanted to enjoy this moment while she could.

They sat on a stack of two-by-fours and watched Mrs. Mundy call the cast to order. While the rehearsal began, Kevin said. "How's school this year, Stephanie?"

*He makes it sound like I'm in the first grade*, Stephanie said to herself. *I'm not a little kid!*

"Okay," she mumbled.

"Are you into sports, or anything?" Kevin asked.

Stephanie shook her head. "I'll be working on the school newspaper, I guess. But that only takes a few hours a week."

"Why don't you work with me on the props and set changes?" Kevin suggested. "We need another set of hands."

Work with Kevin every afternoon? And he was *asking* her to do it? Stephanie felt goosebumps cover her arms. "Well," she began. "Maybe I could."

"Great." Kevin grinned at her. "We want this play to be a real success, don't we? Can't let Maxine and Hal down."

Stephanie gritted her teeth, her brief moment of happiness fading. Maxine again! Couldn't Kevin ever think about anyone else?

# Chapter Ten

Maxine, Hal, and Christine walked across the stage after rehearsal ended. They paused as they saw Kevin and Stephanie.

"Like a ride home, Maxine?" Kevin asked, his smile eager. "My car's in the parking lot."

Stephanie, just behind him, felt the heat rise in her cheeks and knew that she was turning red again. Afraid that someone would notice, she dropped her notebook deliberately and bent to retrieve it, hoping to hide her flushed face.

Unfortunately, Hal made a dive for the notebook at the same time, and they bumped heads. Stephanie gasped from the force of the blow. But at least she had an excuse for looking distracted when she straightened up.

"Sorry, Steph," Hal said. "Just trying to help."

"Since when?" Stephanie retorted. She rubbed her forehead, which still smarted.

It was Hal's turn to redden, glancing at Christine. "Sorry," he repeated.

Stephanie felt a pang of contrition. Was Hal

## STEALING THE SCENE

trying to impress Christine with his good manners? Did he really have a crush on this girl? If so, she wasn't helping matters.

"It's okay, Hal," she said in a polite tone. "Thanks."

Maxine, who had paused to watch this mishap, turned to Kevin.

"Thanks for the offer of a ride," she said, "but I think I'll have to take a rain check. I want to take the bus home with Hal and Stephanie; I need to discuss one of the scenes with Hal."

Kevin looked disappointed. "I guess I'll see you tomorrow then."

Maxine's smile took some of the sting out of her rejection. "Great," she told him.

Kevin looked happier as they walked together through the hall and toward the side exit.

Stephanie frowned. Really, she couldn't figure out Maxine at all. Why did she turn down a ride with Kevin? Didn't she know how nice he was? And that excuse about needing to talk to Hal—didn't she have all night to discuss the play? And the two of them didn't even have a scene together.

But Maxine said good-bye to Kevin outside the school, and Kevin gave the other two a casual wave as he left. "See you," he called.

"Yeah," Stephanie muttered. Discouraged, she trudged after Hal and Maxine toward the bus stop.

The bus was crowded, and no one tried to talk during the ride home. But when they walked up the driveway, Hal joked, "Do you think Tim wins the prize for forgetting the same line three times in a row?"

Maxine and Stephanie both giggled.

"Just wait till opening night," Maxine warned. "Better hope you don't forget any lines."

"Ha," Hal told her. "I'm going to write them on the back of my hand."

"I knew a boy who did that," Maxine admitted. "But he was so nervous and sweated so much that his lines ran together. All he could do was stutter!"

They all laughed.

It was nice to feel a part of things, Stephanie thought, to not be left out.

Inside the house, Stephanie dropped her books on the counter and hurried to claim the phone. She dialed Carol's number.

"There you are," Carol said when she answered. "I called once, but B.J. said no one else was home. What have you been up to?"

"I went to rehearsal, remember?" Stephanie reminded her friend.

"It took that long to get the background for your story?"

"Not really, but Kevin asked me to work backstage with him, so I stayed through the whole rehearsal," Stephanie explained.

There was a short silence. "Do you think that's a smart thing to do?" Carol asked. "I mean, hanging around him when he's drooling over Maxine isn't exactly going to cheer you up."

"I know," Stephanie sighed. "But I just couldn't say no."

"I understand," Carol admitted. "Anyhow, aside from Kevin, I think it's great."

"You *do*?" Stephanie didn't try to hide her surprise. "Why?"

"It's about time you got involved in *something* at school," Carol told her bluntly. "You've been wandering around like a ghost for the last couple of years. What else could you be but miserable?"

"Hey, I did write stories for the paper last year," Stephanie argued.

"Once or twice," Carol snorted. "And then you only appeared in the newspaper office long enough to hand in your story. No, this is great. Maybe I'll come along to rehearsal one day and watch, if I get out of volleyball practice in time."

"It's a deal," Stephanie told her. "But no making eyes at Kevin. I have enough competition as it is."

They both laughed, then Stephanie hung up the phone. It had hardly touched the cradle when it rang again.

"Three guesses who this call is for," Stephanie muttered. She picked up the phone reluctantly. Sure enough, she heard a familiar male voice.

"Is Maxine there?"

Stephanie put the receiver down and headed for the hallway. "Maxine," she yelled. "Telephone!"

Stephanie took her books to her room and curled up on the bed, not emerging until she heard a car in the drive. She was disappointed, however, to see only Eve in the kitchen.

"Where's Dad?" Stephanie said.

"He's working late tonight," Eve said, sounding distracted. "He'll try to get home in time for dinner."

Hal came through the door, his arms full of grocery bags. "Hasn't he found a new assistant yet?" he asked.

Eve shook her head. "He's been interviewing all week, but no luck, so far. I would have stayed, too, but I've had a splitting headache all afternoon."

Hal sat the brown bags on the counter.

B.J., coming in with another armload of sacks, did the same. "Boy, the whole trunk was full," he said. "We ought to have enough food tonight."

Maxine came into the kitchen. Peering into the first bag, she began to empty the contents, taking a handful of cans and boxes to stack on the pantry shelves. "With you two around, I wouldn't bet on it," she said.

B.J. stuck out his tongue at his sister.

"Now, now," Maxine reprimanded him sweetly.

B.J. looked like he wanted to punch Maxine, but a glance from his mother prevented the quarrel from escalating.

"What's for dinner?" Hal asked.

Eve nodded toward the counter. "I bought a family sized—that means *big*—package of pork chops. How does that sound?"

"Good," Hal said. "Grilled, with pineapple slices on top."

"Boring," B.J. objected. "Batter and fry them."

"Too greasy," Maxine pointed out. "Let's have something more *haute cuisine*. Why not stuff them with mushroom and onion dressing?"

"I don't like onions," Stephanie said.

"You don't like anything." B.J. shook his head.

"That's it!" Eve startled them all by the shrillness in her tone. "That's it, I give up!" She dropped the package of meat back on the counter, and, one hand on her temple, looked sternly at each of them.

"I've had it with all of you—I feel like a short-order cook! If you can't agree on anything, you figure out the menu. And I don't mean peanut-butter sandwiches. Then *you* can cook it. Just let me know when dinner's ready. I'm going to lie down."

"But we don't know how!" B.J. blurted, staring at his mother in surprise.

"Cookbooks are on the shelf," Eve answered. "Better get started." She pulled off her apron, dropped it on the back of a chair and stalked out of the kitchen.

"Good grief." Stephanie stared after her. "What was that all about?"

Maxine's answer sounded sharp. "You should know."

"Meaning?" Stephanie knew she'd raised her voice, but it was hard not to shout when Maxine looked down her nose at her in that irritating, superior manner.

"Be quiet, both of you," Hal told them. "It's true, nobody here likes to eat the same thing."

"So?" Stephanie still felt aggrieved. "Can we help it if we don't like some foods?"

"It wouldn't hurt you to try something new," Maxine told her.

"That goes for you, too!" Stephanie retorted.

"Hey," Hal interjected. "Save your energy for the cooking." He grinned at them. "Who wants the apron?"

B.J. shook his head at all this commotion. "Tough luck," he said. "Call me when it's done." He started toward the doorway.

"Wait right there!" Maxine grabbed her brother by the back of his shirt. "You don't get out of it that easily!"

"Yeah," Stephanie agreed.

"But I don't know how to cook," B.J. argued.

"Then you can learn," Maxine told him. "This is an equal-opportunity kitchen, little brother."

B.J. made a face and he squared his shoulders, but he resigned.

"How are we going to do this?" Hal asked. "I'm willing, but I'm not particularly able."

"You can say that again." Stephanie pretended to shudder. "I've eaten some of Hal's dinners."

Hal looked offended. "They weren't *that* bad."

"We'll find out," Maxine said. "Okay, we're dividing this dinner up. Who wants to do the pork chops?"

The two boys looked at each other.

"Oh, all right," Maxine said, "I'll take those.

## STEALING THE SCENE

Better not destroy the main course by giving it to you guys. That leaves potatoes or rice or noodles, vegetables, salad and bread."

"Why so much?" B.J. demanded.

"It's what Mom would cook," Maxine reminded him.

"Okay, I'll take the bread," B.J. volunteered, brightening.

"Ha," Maxine looked at him suspiciously. "If you think you're going to just open a fresh loaf, you're out of luck. You also get to fix a salad. And wash your hands before you start."

B.J. headed for the sink. "Bossy big sisters," he mumbled under his breath.

Maxine paid no attention. "What about you two?" she demanded.

Hal looked at his sister. "Heads or tails?"

"I'll do the potatoes," Stephanie decided. "Even you can't ruin vegetables—I hope."

They all set to work. Stephanie rummaged in the potato bin and came out with a handful of potatoes. "I need to get to the sink," she told Maxine, who was rinsing the pork chops under running water.

"In a minute," Maxine told her, "when I'm done. If you scrub those now, you'll get dirt on my pork chops."

Stephanie wrinkled her nose. As she waited for Maxine, however, it occurred to Stephanie that there might be an easier way. She put the potatoes back and looked into the pantry, coming out with a packaged mix of scalloped potatoes.

*This doesn't sound too hard*, she thought. She measured milk and water into a saucepan and put it on the stovetop to boil. She took out margarine, then read the rest of the directions on the back of the package.

Too late, Stephanie discovered she was supposed to boil the water, but not the milk. She ran to the stove, but discovered her mixture already bubbling.

"What's wrong?" Maxine asked.

"Nothing," Stephanie said, unwilling to admit to her mistake. She picked the skin off the boiled milk, and got the dish ready to put into the oven.

"How am I going to broil the porkchops if you're using the oven to bake?" Maxine demanded.

"I have to cook my potatoes!" Stephanie answered.

They glared at each other for a moment, then Maxine shook her head.

"Oh well," she said. "I suppose there must be a way to cook the pork chops at the same time." She went to the cookbook and began to flip the pages.

Meanwhile, Hal took a fresh stalk of cauliflower, washed it, then stared at the hard base, his expression perplexed. "Do we really eat this?"

B.J. looked over his shoulder. "That stuff looks like it's meant for cows," he said, "not for people."

Maxine came to their aid. "Cut off the florets," she told Hal. "You don't eat the bottom part."

Hal took the cutting board and knife and gingerly began his operation, looking as nervous as a novice surgeon.

"Ouch," he muttered, cutting himself. He looked at his small wound.

"Hey, don't bleed on the cauliflower," Stephanie told him.

"Thank you, Florence Nightingale," Hal quipped. He stopped work long enough to wrap a plastic bandage around his finger, then returned to the cutting board.

"Now what?" he asked the rest of them. "Just put it on to boil?"

"Use the microwave," Maxine advised. "Cooks quicker, and saves vitamins. But you'll have to change pans; that one's metal."

"I knew that," Hal said defensively. "Hey, what about some fresh mushrooms on top? I saw a circle of toadstools in the backyard—"

They all stared at him with expressions of horror. "Are you kidding?" Maxine demanded.

"Want us to turn purple and die?" B.J. looked horrified.

"Hal, you wouldn't!" Stephanie gasped.

"Hey, I was just kidding," Hal told them. "Relax, okay?"

Stephanie decided to keep an eye on him, just in case.

Maxine had located a recipe for baked pork chops. "This calls for onions and sage to flavor the meat," she said. She waved one hand at Stephanie before she could protest. "I know, I know. I'll leave out this onions, but how about the sage? Do you like that?"

"I don't know," Stephanie confessed. She felt obliged to make a considerate gesture, too. "I guess I can try it."

"Good." Maxine prepared the meat quickly, and popped it into the oven beside the dish of potatoes.

"Now what?"

"B.J.'s got to make the salad," Maxine reminded her brother. "I'll set the table."

"I'll make some iced tea," Stephanie said, not to be outdone. Besides, she thought, that way she'd be sure that the lemons were put on the side.

When they finally gathered around the table, the dinner didn't look too bad. The pork chops were nicely browned, and Stephanie's scalloped potatoes smelled good. Hal had managed to slightly overcook the cauliflower, and the cheese soup he'd tried to use as a sauce had hardened in the microwave.

"Just think of it as slightly chewy," Hal advised them. "Good exercise for the teeth."

Maxine had gone to call her mother. When Eve came into the kitchen, the lines of tension in her forehead had disappeared. She looked at the full table.

"Looks good, kids."

She took a seat just as Don came through the front door.

"Something smells good," he called. "I'll be

right there." He hung up his jacket and joined them at the table.

Stephanie felt a moment of pride. "We did it all ourselves," she told her father. "Eve had a headache."

"That was nice of you guys," Don told them.

The four teenagers exchanged slightly guilty glances, but Eve smiled and didn't say a word. Maxine handed the platter of pork chops around the table, and everyone began to eat.

Stephanie took a helping of B.J.'s salad, staring suspiciously at the mixture. "What'd you put in this?" she demanded.

"The usual stuff," B.J. assured her. "Lettuce, tomatoes, olives, tortilla chips."

"Tortilla chips?"

"I like them." B.J. looked defensive.

They ate for a few minutes in silence.

"Very good," Eve told them.

"Not bad, if I do say so," Hal agreed, "though I won't mind if Eve takes over tomorrow. She's still the best cook around here. And maybe we can remember not to gripe so much."

He looked at his sister.

Stephanie frowned, but then nodded. "Okay," she agreed.

"We can help out more, too," Maxine suggested. "Mom's been working hard at the marina. It's a lot easier when you don't have to cook the whole meal by yourself."

"Good point," Hal agreed, trying to saw an overlarge piece of lettuce into chewable proportions with his fork. "Just don't let B.J. make the salad again. This looks like dinner for my rabbits."

"Fat chance!" B.J. tossed an olive at him, and Hal ducked.

For the first time, they all laughed at the same joke.

# Chapter Eleven

"I pray thee, gentle mortal, sing again, mine ear is much enamour'd of thy note...," Christine, the bemused fairy queen, murmured. "I love thee."

"Methinks, mis-mis-mistress," Hal stammered, "you should have, should have—"

"Little reason for that," Mrs. Mundy prompted impatiently at rehearsal Monday afternoon. "Really, Hal. I thought you promised to have this scene memorized by today."

"I do. I mean, I did," Hal sputtered. "It's just—"

"It's okay, Mrs. Mundy," Christine told the teacher. "I'll go over this scene again with Hal while you're directing the next act."

The two of them retreated to the back of the auditorium, while Maxine, Anne, Tim, and John began the next scene.

"What's gotten into Hal?" Stephanie whispered to Kevin as they watched from the side of the stage. "I went over that scene with him yesterday, and he knew every word. How could he have forgotten it overnight?"

"Christine isn't his little sister," Kevin pointed out.

Stephanie stared at him. Had everyone noticed Hal's crush?

"Just a wild guess." Kevin grinned. "Come on, let me show you the set designs one of the art students did for the play."

Stephanie followed him back to the drama room, where Kevin took a set of drawings off the teacher's desk and held them up for Stephanie to see.

"Mrs. Mundy went over this with me before you got here. The sets are simple, which is just as well, since you and I are the ones who get to move them around. This is the duke's palace, just a backdrop and some white columns, decorated with silk flowers for the coming wedding. We use this for the first scene. The second scene is Quince's house—he's one of the workmen, like Bottom—Mrs. Mundy's going to do it in front of the curtain with no scenery. It's a short scene, but it gives *us* time to run around behind the closed curtain, taking away the palace scene and putting up the forest."

"It sounds kind of funny—*making* a forest," Stephanie said. She smiled at Kevin.

"I know. We drag all the silk trees and potted flowers out and arrange them for the first scene in act two, then rearrange them for another part of the wood in scene three. Same for act three, and the first scene in act four. Then there's another short scene in front of the curtain at Quince's house while we pull the woods back and put the 'palace' in place again for the last act."

"We're going to be busy," Stephanie realized.

"Right," Kevin told her. "And we have to be very quiet, so the audience won't hear us. Rubber-soled shoes are a necessity."

Stephanie giggled.

"Here's our list of props." Kevin brought out another piece of paper. "A purple silk flower for Puck to work his magic love potion with, swords for Lysander and Demetrius to fight with, and the donkey's head for your brother to wear when he's under Puck's spell."

"Poor Hal," Stephanie murmured. "I didn't know we had so much to do. This is going to be fun. We really do have an important job, don't we?"

"Of course," Kevin said. "Where would the actors be if the swords weren't ready for the big fight scene?"

"I know where *we'd* be—out of a job!" Stephanie laughed. "Mrs. Mundy would have our heads."

"That's okay," Kevin told her, "I have a replacement ready." He picked up the donkey's mask and tried it on for size, wiggling the long ears with one hand.

Stephanie laughed again. She felt blissfully happy. If only Kevin would pay attention to her like this all the time, instead of mooning over Maxine.

"Come on," Kevin said. "Let's get back to the stage. We have columns to build."

"Yes, sir!" Stephanie saluted smartly.

"Okay, people—that's it for today!" Mrs. Mundy called out, announcing the end of rehearsal. "See you tomorrow," she said, putting her script and notebook back into her tote bag. "And Hal, work on those lines."

"I will," Hal promised, absently kicking something on the stage with his foot.

As the cast members began to leave, Kevin put down his hammer. "Hey, we've got two columns completed. You really work well with a hammer and saw," he said warmly to Stephanie. "Let's finish the rest tomorrow."

She nodded, but Kevin had already turned to look at Maxine who was collecting her books from the end of the stage. He waved at her.

"Hey," he called. "Want a ride home today? How about an ice-cream cone on the way?"

Stephanie put down the wood frame she'd been holding, restraining herself from throwing it across the stage. Maxine again! Just when things seemed to be going well between Kevin and herself, Maxine always reappeared. Talk about stealing the scene!

Yet Maxine didn't seem eager to accept Kevin's offer. "I don't know," she began. For a second she glanced over at Stephanie. Stephanie lowered her head quickly so Maxine wouldn't see her unhappy expression, pretending to inspect the column she and Kevin had just completed.

## STEALING THE SCENE    111

"Hal and Stephanie—" Maxine went on. "I'd meant to go home with them."

"They can come along," Kevin offered. "Feel like getting some ice cream, guys?"

Stephanie didn't know what to say. Which was worse—turning down a chance to be with Kevin, or torturing herself as she watched Kevin adore her stepsister?

While she hesitated, Hal answered, "Sure, we'll come. If you're buying, I'll have a triple scoop."

Kevin and Maxine made their way toward the exit. "Come on, guys," Kevin called.

"Having fun?" Hal asked his sister as they followed Kevin and Maxine out the door. "Working on the set, I mean?"

"I was," Stephanie grumbled. "Until he called me a *guy*."

Sitting in the ice-cream shop, Stephanie ate her double dip of strawberry slowly, while she tried not to listen to the chairman of the Maxine Smyth Fan Club.

"You're doing a great job with your part," Kevin told Maxine. "I think you're a born actress!"

"Well—," Maxine began, taking a dainty bite of her pralines and cream.

"You're certainly effective in the love scenes," Stephanie interrupted, unable to resist. "But then, I guess you've had lots of practice."

Maxine raised her brows, frowning, and Kevin looked shocked.

"With all your acting experience, I mean," Stephanie went on, her tone innocent.

"Thanks," Maxine told her stepsister dryly. "But I'm not sure our director agrees. Mrs. Mundy took us apart during act three today."

"It wasn't your fault," Hal objected. "Tim and John kept fighting with their swords instead of listening to her directions."

"They were awfully funny, though," Stephanie said, happy to see the conversation move away from Maxine. "They'll get a lot of laughs. All that confusion over being in love with the same girl, first Hermia, then Helena."

"That's okay in a play," Hal said. "Not much like real life, though, do you think? I mean, two people in love with the same person—that's so corny."

Stephanie stared at the tile floor, beginning to wish she'd hadn't agreed to come. This was too much!

"Shakespeare's right about one thing," Kevin said. "A guy always seems to be more interested in a girl when she's not as interested in him." He grinned at Maxine.

"'Cupid is a knavish lad, thus to make poor females mad,'" Maxine quoted from the play, ignoring Kevin's suggestive comment. "And not always just females, right, Hal?"

Hal blushed. "Probably," he agreed. "What do you think, Steph?"

Stephanie concentrated on her ice cream, afraid she'd blush, too. "Probably."

# Chapter Twelve

For the next week and a half, rehearsals went rather smoothly. Stephanie and Kevin completed the stage settings, collected all their props, and practiced changing the scenes.

"How's it going?" Carol asked Thursday at lunch. "Are you dying of frustration, seeing your favorite hunk every day?"

"Smart alec." Stephanie threw a piece of roll at her friend. "We've gotten to be real friends, I think. Unfortunately, the only thing he notices about me is my skill with a hammer. It's been fun, though."

"Except that he's still crazy about Maxine," Carol finished for her.

"Right," Stephanie sighed. "You'd think he might look at me just once, but, no!"

"I told Mrs. Mundy I'd sell tickets this weekend, but when we close the box office, I'm going to slip into the auditorium and watch the play. Do you think it'll be good?"

"Yeah. Maxine lives and breathes her part,"

Stephanie told her friend. "Not much chance she'll forget a word. As for Hal, I don't know. He does fine with the funny parts of his role, but when he has to act with Christine, he forgets everything. I think he likes her."

"Really?"

"But don't repeat that," Stephanie said quickly. "He'd kill me if it got back to her."

"I won't say a word," Carol promised "But she might not mind. Hal's pretty cute, you know."

"He is?" Stephanie looked up in surprise.

Carol laughed. "Just because he's your brother doesn't mean he can't be good-looking."

"Ha, ha." The bell rang sharply, and they both picked up their lunch trays. "Dress rehearsal tonight," Stephanie said. "I hope it goes well."

But when they gathered in the auditorium after school, the dress rehearsal seemed doomed from the start. During the first set change, Stephanie knocked over one of the columns for the duke's palace, and the resulting bang seemed to echo through the auditorium. Mrs. Mundy frowned, and shook her head.

One of the ears from Hal's donkey mask fell off during a love scene with Christine, and Hal turned so red Christine forgot her own lines, giggling.

Even the usually unflappable Maxine forgot a line, and had to be cued by the drama teacher.

"I don't believe it," Stephanie murmured backstage. "Maxine missing a cue?"

## STEALING THE SCENE

"She's just nervous," Kevin said quickly. "She'll be all right tomorrow night."

Stephanie frowned, wishing he didn't always jump to her stepsister's defense.

"Thanks a bunch," she fumed.

"What?" Kevin looked at her in surprise.

"When I knocked over the column, you laughed your head off at me," Stephanie told him hotly. "You made as much noise as I did, and Mrs. Mundy only yelled at me!"

"Hey, I'm sorry." Kevin's tone was soothing. "But it was funny, admit it."

Despite herself, Stephanie grinned. "I guess so."

"And we'll all do okay tomorrow, just wait and see," Kevin predicted, optimistic as always.

"I hope so," Stephanie told him. "I'm nervous already."

Kevin drove all three of them home, and the whole carload was unusually quiet. Even Hal didn't seem to have enough energy to joke, and Maxine appeared lost in thought. She barely even remembered to thank Kevin for the ride.

By dinnertime, their nervousness had resulted in frazzled tempers all around. The two boys joined Stephanie at the table, while Eve sliced a savory pot roast and poured gravy into a gravyboat.

"Don should be home soon," Eve said, setting the platter of food in the middle of the table. "Where's Maxine? Isn't she eating?"

"Don't know," Hal said, taking a large piece of meat. "I told her dinner was ready."

"All right, where's my red dress?" Maxine demanded, appearing in the kitchen doorway, her green eyes bright with anger. "I hung it on the back of the bathroom door, and now it's not there!"

"I moved it." B.J. shrugged. "It was in the way. Why didn't you put it in your room? You always yell at me when I leave *my* clothes lying around."

Maxine shook her head. "I had to steam my red velvet dress to get the wrinkles out. It's the prettiest costume I wear in the whole play—I spend most of the acts in that plain green dress. What did you do with it?"

"Stuck it inside the linen closet," B.J. confessed. "It was closest."

"The linen closet?" Maxine sounded outraged. "If you've wrinkled my costume, you're dead."

"So put it in your room," B.J. said. "And keep it out of our way."

"I don't have enough space in my closet," Maxine argued. "If you'd move some of your stuff and give me part of your closet—"

"Dresses in my closet?" B.J. looked stubborn. "No way."

"Besides," Hal pointed out, "we don't have any room to spare, either. With all B.J.'s junk in my room—"

"My baseball gear is not junk!" B.J. sounded insulted. "And who said it was just *your* room?"

"Okay, *our* room," Hal grumbled. "I should

say your room. You're taking up two thirds of the space!"

"How about if we draw a line down the middle?" B.J. suggested. "No, why don't you just move me into the garage?"

"How about the rabbit pen?" Hal grinned.

Stephanie turned indignantly to Maxine, sudden realization making her frown. "Do you mean that I couldn't get into the bathroom for the last hour because you were steaming your dress? It's bad enough that you hog the bathroom all the time—"

"I do not!" Maxine said.

"Do, too," Stephanie persisted. "You spend so much time getting your hair fixed just so, and putting on all that makeup—"

"Wouldn't hurt you to try it sometime," Maxine said coolly.

"Now, girls," Eve tried to interrupt.

But Stephanie almost choked on her pot roast. "Why, you—" she sputtered.

"Besides, what else can I do? I don't have a mirror in my room," Maxine went on.

"I've been meaning to get you a mirror, Maxine," Eve said, "but I've been so busy, between the house and working at the marina with Don, I just haven't gotten to it."

"It won't do much good," Maxine grumbled. "I still won't have any space in that tiny excuse for a room."

"If you did, you'd just fill it up with makeup and clothes." Stephanie glared across the table.

"You're just as bad as B.J. with his baseball junk."

"It is not junk," B.J. repeated, frowning at them all.

"Besides—," Maxine began.

"What is this—World War Three?" Don Smith, his hands full of mail from the hall table, appeared in the doorway.

"It's not my fault," Stephanie told her father. "Maxine always hogs the bathroom."

"And B.J. takes up the whole bedroom," Hal mumbled, looking sheepish under his father's stern gaze.

"Nothing like feeling part of the family." Maxine's comment dripped sarcasm.

Don looked from the angry group of teenagers to Eve, who was obviously upset. "The van was the easy part," he said, almost to himself. "Now the house doesn't have enough room for everyone, either."

"Meaning?" Hal demanded, staring at his father.

"Meaning I think Eve and I will start looking at houses," Don told them flatly. "I think we need a bigger house."

"Great!" B.J. applauded this idea. "Can I have my own room?"

"I need a decent-sized bedroom with *large* closets," Maxine urged.

Hal looked surprised, but not displeased. "How big a house can we get?" he asked.

Don looked at Eve. "We'll have to see what we can afford."

Eve nodded. "Don't start expecting a castle," she warned them. "Now everybody settle down and eat your dinner."

The other three dug into their pot roast and vegetables willingly. But Stephanie stared down at her plate, her appetite abruptly gone.

Leave her bedroom, leave behind the house that she'd shared with her mother? Forever?

Stephanie swallowed hard, feeling tears in her eyes. It was all because of Maxine and B.J. All they had brought the Smith family was one problem after another.

She stood up abruptly and threw down her napkin. "I'm not hungry," she said.

"She's nervous about opening night," she heard Hal say as she left the kitchen. "So am I. I bet I won't be able to sleep at all tonight."

*Ha,* Stephanie thought. Who cared about the dumb play when she was losing the only home she'd ever known?

But when Friday night arrived, Stephanie discovered she was almost as jittery as Hal and Maxine, which was saying plenty. Maxine was so nervous that she dropped her eye liner down the toilet and almost cried.

"I have to have my eye liner!" she shrieked. "I can't go on stage with naked eyes!"

"I thought you didn't put on your stage make-up until you got backstage," Stephanie said, curious despite her resolve to avoid her troublesome stepsister.

"We do," Maxine agreed. "But I'm still not

walking into the school building looking like this." She fought back a sob.

Hal looked through the open doorway to see what was going on. "Did you hurt yourself?"

"I ruined my eye liner," Maxine told him. "And no wise cracks—I need it!"

"Mrs. Mundy has a whole cabinet full of stage makeup," Hal reminded her. "Don't you think she'll have what you need?"

"You're right," Maxine said, looking calmer. "I wasn't thinking. I'll wear sunglasses until I get inside."

"That's okay, I'm a nervous wreck, too." Hal grinned weakly. "What if my ears fall off again? And how do I get through the big love scene when every time I look at Christine, my mind goes completely blank?"

"Don't look at her," Maxine advised. "It's not the usual practice in a love scene, but if she bothers you that much, look over her shoulder. The audience won't be able to tell the difference, and maybe you can remember your lines that way."

"Thanks," Hal muttered. "I'll try it." He headed back toward his bedroom.

"Why do I have to dress up?" B.J. demanded, struggling with his tie. "It's not like this is a *real* play."

"Thanks a bunch," Hal told him.

Eve, who had heard the comment, too, spoke from the hallway. "It won't hurt you to look nice," she said.

"Who said?" B.J. asked, looking pained.

"And get a move on, it's almost time to leave," Hal reminded the younger boy. "Maxine and Steph and I have to be there early, remember."

"Everybody in this whole family tells me what to do," B.J. grumbled.

Ten minutes later, they all piled into the big silver van and drove to the high school. Maxine, Hal, and Stephanie left the others at their seats in the auditorium and hurried to the back entrance. Mrs. Mundy was in the outer alcove, checking off her list of actors and actresses, making sure everyone arrived in good time.

Maxine headed straight for the dressing room, carrying her two costumes wrapped carefully in plastic, and Hal followed her back to the boys' dressing room across the hall.

Stephanie checked out the stage. She and Kevin had arranged the set yesterday, setting out the white columns and hanging the floral decorations. Everything was still in place. The big crimson stage curtains were closed, so she tiptoed across the stage. The silk trees and potted flowers were crowded in the wings, ready for the first scene change.

The prop table at the side of the stage, out of sight of the audience, had all the essential props ready for the actors, and the extra costumes would hang on the rack just outside both dressing rooms.

"Looks good," Stephanie mumbled, checking her watch. "Only twenty minutes till curtain. Where is Kevin?"

There was no way she could change the sets all

by herself. Besides, his grin would calm the jittery feeling inside her stomach.

Stephanie walked up and down behind the set, wondering if Kevin had been delayed. Surely his car hadn't broken down, tonight of all nights? Or, even worse, had he been in an accident?

Stephanie shivered. "Don't be silly," she scolded herself. But Kevin was never late. Where was he?

Looking across the empty stage, Stephanie suddenly saw his tall form, standing just outside the girls' dressing room. Maxine stood beside him, and she looked anxious.

Kevin said something to Maxine in a low voice—Stephanie couldn't make out the words—but she could imagine his soothing tone.

Then he bent and kissed Maxine on the lips.

"That's it!" Stephanie shrieked.

# Chapter Thirteen

Without thinking, Stephanie ran across the stage. She stopped in front of the embracing couple. Maxine frowned and moved away from Kevin.

Kevin looked surprised. "What's wrong, Stephanie? Is it something about the set?"

*What's wrong?* Were boys born with oatmeal for brains? *It's not the set, it's this scene!*

"You just have to do it, don't you?" Stephanie asked Maxine. "Take away everything I care about! I'd just as soon live with a rattlesnake as have you for a sister!" she yelled.

Maxine's eyes glinted with anger, but her expression remained controlled. "Lower your voice," she said sharply. "The audience will hear you."

"I don't care," Stephanie began, heedless of the crowded auditorium just beyond the closed curtains. This time she was going to tell Maxine exactly what she thought of her!

But just then Mrs. Mundy came running across

123

the stage, glancing over the carefully arranged stage setting.

"The set looks very nice, Kevin, Stephanie," the teacher said briskly. "Stephanie, be careful tonight. No more falling columns."

Stephanie nodded, forced to bite back her angry tirade.

The drama teacher seemed too absorbed with the play to notice the tension between the girls. "Maxine, where's John? Don't let him forget in your first scene—"

Mrs. Mundy swept Maxine into the dressing room, and Stephanie was left alone on the stage with Kevin.

She stared down at her worn Nikes, unable to look him in the eye. She'd done it this time—humiliated herself completely. Now he would know how she felt about him and would probably be repulsed, or even worse, amused.

"I'll check the trees again," she mumbled, and rushed back across the stage to hide herself in the 'forest.'

Once out of Kevin's sight, she put her hands to her face, still trembling with frustrated anger. "It's always Maxine causing problems and getting all the attention," she muttered to herself.

"That was pretty stupid," a male voice said.

Stephanie practically jumped. She turned to find Hal looking at her. He had donned his brown costume and his face was covered with heavy stage makeup.

"What do you mean?"

"I saw that little tantrum," Hal told her bluntly. "Why don't you grow up, Steph? Face it, Maxine hasn't done anything except be herself. Can you blame her for being pretty and talented?"

"No," Stephanie protested. "But Kevin—"

"No one can steal something you don't have," Hal went on. "You never had Kevin. And you're not going to have any other friends if you keep acting like this."

Stephanie bit her lip. "I just wanted Kevin to like me, that's all," she mumbled.

Hal looked more sympathetic, but he still shook his head. "You can't *make* a boy like you," he told her. "But if you keep acting this way, you can sure convince Kevin to *dislike* you. Better think about it, Steph."

"Places for the first scene," Mrs. Mundy whispered from across the stage. "Curtain's going up in one minute."

"Oh, no!" Hal gulped. He seemed to be suffering from a sudden attack of stage fright. "Cross your fingers, Steph. I'm afraid I'll forget my lines."

"You'll do fine," Stephanie assured him. "Go break a leg—no, I take that back. Knowing you, you just might. But I will cross my fingers. Toes, too."

Hal hurried off. Stephanie stepped back into the wings, and the curtains rolled back.

Juan, the boy who played the duke Theseus, and Georgette, resplendent in a gold satin dress as his queenly fiancée, walked out on the stage, and the play began.

Stephanie remembered Georgette's dissatisfaction with her role. Sure enough, Georgette did only have a line or two before Maxine, as Hermia, came onto the stage. Joining her were John and Tim, her two suitors, and a stocky boy who played Hermia's father.

If Stephanie's outburst had upset her stepsister, it didn't show. Maxine spoke her lines with ease and conviction as she argued with her "father" about which man she wished to marry.

"She's good," Stephanie murmured. "She really is."

As Maxine and John, now alone on the stage, lamented that "the course of true love never did run smooth," and plotted how they would run away to be married in another city, Stephanie almost forgot her anger.

It was all true, just as Shakespeare had written it; People never seemed to love the person who loved them back. She liked Kevin, who liked Maxine, who liked—who knew?

But Stephanie forgot her musings as the scene came to an end. She saw Hal, with the other workmen, about to walk out in front of the curtain. Hal still looked nervous, and she saw him gulp. But she had no time to watch her brother's stage debut, because it was time for the first set change. She had to face Kevin!

Stephanie felt her face burn with embarrassment, but luckily the stage lights had been dimmed behind the closed curtains. Maybe he wouldn't notice her red face. She grabbed a column and began to carry it off the stage.

"Quick," Kevin whispered as he grabbed another column. "We don't have much time."

With only occasional whispers, they streaked across the stage, removing the first set and putting the trees and flowers into place.

"Ready?" Mrs. Mundy hissed at them.

Kevin nodded. He and Stephanie dashed off the stage as the curtains slid open again.

Stephanie found herself standing in the wings as the fairy band began the next scene. But Stephanie couldn't concentrate on Puck's mischief; she was too aware of Kevin at her elbow.

She took a deep breath. Might as well get it over with, just in case there was any chance Kevin might forgive her.

"I'm sorry about what I said, before," Stephanie whispered. She didn't dare meet Kevin's gorgeous blue eyes.

To her surprise, Kevin grinned. "That's okay. Maxine told me you two had a fight before you left home. She said she stayed in the bathroom too long getting ready; it was her fault. But she was probably nervous about tonight, Stephanie. Don't blame her too much."

He chuckled quietly. "You sure have a hot temper, though. Remind me not to get on your bad side!"

Stephanie couldn't smile back. She felt a rush of conflicting emotions—anger that Kevin always took Maxine's side, mixed with relief that Maxine had made an excuse for her. Kevin still didn't realize that *he* was the real reason for Stephanie's anger. She bit her lip and didn't answer.

As the play continued, she and Kevin stayed busy, making sure the actors got the right props and shifting the sets. She handed Hal his donkey's head halfway through the play, trying not to giggle as he slipped it on.

"Like a bite of hay?"

"Very funny," Hal told her. "Cut the wisecracks, or this donkey may bite *you*."

He headed back to take his place, ready for his next entrance.

Hal was doing a good job with his part, Stephanie thought, listening to the hearty laughter from the audience that his clowning evoked. And during his last scene with Christine, when she held him in her arms, Stephanie was ready to bet that Hal's face, beneath the mask, had turned beet red. Would he ever get enough nerve to tell Christine how he felt about her? she wondered.

During the fourth act, Kevin whispered, "Where's the cape the duke wears in the next scene?"

"Outside the dressing room, I think," Stephanie told him. "I'll check, just to be sure."

She left Kevin and tiptoed back to the dressing rooms, located just behind the stage. Most of the actors had already made their last change, but she heard two girls whispering and giggling in the girls' dressing room. It was Georgette and her friend Tina, and Stephanie snuck a look at them from the edge of the door. They were holding

## STEALING THE SCENE 129

Maxine's red dress, the one she wore in the last scene of the play.

"Let's hide it," Georgette was saying. "We could put it in the boys' wardrobe, behind those old costumes. Maxine will positively die if she can't find it. She'll have to wear the same old dress in the party scene, and she'll be so mad, she'll forget half her lines! Serves her right for taking my part!"

The two girls giggled again.

Stephanie stepped back into the shadows, out of sight. She had to fight back a surge of laughter. *I can just see Maxine's face,* she told herself. *Boy, will she be steamed! She loves that dress.*

For just a moment, Stephanie shook with silent laughter. She stayed very still as the two girls slipped out of the dressing room, still giggling, and headed for the wings.

Then, somehow, her own amusement faded. What right did Georgette and Tina have to spoil Maxine's final act? Perhaps Maxine got the part that Georgette had wanted, but she'd won it fair and square, hadn't she? You couldn't blame Maxine for being pretty and talented, Stephanie thought, then realized she was echoing Hal's comment. Well, it was true. Just because Maxine got the role—or the boy—she wanted, it wasn't fair to stab her in the back. Maxine had worked hard to make her performance letter perfect, and no one should be allowed to mess her up, not now.

"There's no way they're going to ruin the whole last act of the play," Stephanie muttered.

"Not after all the hard work we put into this thing."

Stephanie hurried into the dressing room, going straight to the boys' wardrobe and digging through the old costumes in the back. She found the scarlet dress and pulled it out, smoothing the heavy folds and hanging it back in place on the rack by the door. She picked up the duke's cloak, too, to take back to the stage.

When she looked up, she saw Kevin standing in the doorway.

"What happened?" he asked in a low voice. "What was Maxine's dress doing in the boys' locker?"

"Somebody was playing a joke, I think," Stephanie told him briefly.

He grinned at her. "Good work, Stephanie."

His words made Stephanie feel good. For once, she knew she'd done the right thing.

The last act went smoothly and Stephanie was thrilled to see Georgette look disappointed when Maxine came onstage in her proper, beautiful costume.

When the curtains closed for the last time, then reopened for the curtain calls, the cast received hearty applause. Hal, to his obvious surprise, got especially loud cheers.

"You were great, Hal," Stephanie called from the wings as she clapped along with the audience.

Hal, grinning, took an extra bow.

Maxine got a big hand, too. And when she took her individual bow, Kevin ran onstage to hand her a bouquet of red roses, wrapped in white paper.

Maxine, her eyes bright, gave him a luminous smile.

Kevin hurried offstage as the rest of the cast took turns stepping forward into the spotlight.

"That's why I was late getting here," he told Stephanie. "Stopped at the florist. And this is for you."

It was a single red rosebud, wrapped in paper and tied with a white ribbon. Stephanie felt a thrill leap through her as she took the flower.

"For the best stagehand in the play," Kevin told her. "We make a good team, Stephanie."

She grinned back at him, feeling both happy and proud. "We do, don't we?"

Out front, the audience continued to clap. "Director!" someone called.

Mrs. Mundy took a bow, then she waved for the entire stage crew to join her onstage and share in the applause.

Stephanie hesitated, and Kevin grabbed her hand. "Come on, you deserve it."

They stepped onto the stage, just behind the line of actors and actresses. Maxine, in the center of the line, moved back and opened a space for them to join the front row.

Stephanie stepped shyly into the spotlight, Kevin on her right, Maxine on her left, and Hal just beyond, and they all joined hands for one final bow. In the audience, Stephanie saw her dad, Eve and B.J. smiling up at them.

Maxine caught Stephanie's eye. "We did it!"

she murmured beneath the last wave of applause. They shared a quick grin.

Then the row of actors and crew stepped back, and the curtain rolled across the stage once more.

What a relief—the first performance was over, and everything had gone well. But Stephanie's euphoria didn't last long. The line of cast and crew began to break up into laughing, talking groups. She was too close to Maxine not to overhear Kevin when he stepped forward and whispered, "Maybe we can continue that kiss after we're through cleaning up?"

But Maxine shook her head firmly.

"I do like you, you know that," Maxine told him. "And that kiss—I know you were only trying to make me feel better because I was so nervous about opening night. But we're just friends, Kevin. That's the only way I'll go on seeing you." She turned abruptly and headed for the dressing room.

Kevin seemed perplexed. "I don't understand her," he complained. "Smiling at me one minute, pulling away the next. I'm not sure she understands herself."

He looked at Stephanie, who stared back at him wordlessly.

"But I don't give up easily," Kevin went on. "Maybe you could put in a good word for me, once in a while."

Stephanie thought she would die when she heard Kevin's request. Play matchmaker for Maxine and Kevin? Could her life possibly get any more complicated?

But when Kevin smiled at her like that, what could she say? "Maybe," she mumbled. This was obviously one drama that was not over yet, no matter what Maxine said.

"You're a doll." Kevin grinned down at her. "Better get started on the cleanup." He turned away.

Stephanie sighed and started to follow him. *A doll,* she thought to herself. *Well, it's better than being called a guy—I guess.*

Just then someone grabbed her from behind in a big bear hug. Stephanie gasped in surprise, struggling to see over her shoulder. It was Hal, grinning from ear to ear.

"The play was a hit," Hal crowed as he released her, still beaming. "And I didn't forget a single line!"

"You were great," Stephanie told her brother, forgetting her own problems as she smiled at him.

"We all were—me, Maxine, and you, too. Where would the drama crew *be* without us?" Hal joked. "I sure hope Dad and Eve don't find a new house in a different school district. Mrs. Mundy's got to be the best drama coach ever. And besides, what about Christine—I mean, uh, *all* our friends at school?"

Stephanie's smile vanished. "Give up our home? Our high school? No way. We've got to stop them, Hal!"

"How?" he demanded. "We do need more room, Steph. Maybe we can find a larger house in our own neighborhood."

Stephanie couldn't say anything. She felt like she was going to start crying. Just when things seemed to be settling down and improving—wham! Another change in her life, another change that would move her farther and farther away from the memory of her mother.

Hal patted her on the shoulder. "It's going to be okay," he told her. "Don't worry."

Stephanie wasn't convinced, but she didn't know how to make him understand. *It's up to me,* she told herself. *I have to stop this move, somehow!*

## ABOUT THE AUTHOR

Cheryl Zach's son, daughter, and two stepsons have taught her a great deal about blended families. Born in Tennessee, this former "army brat" has also lived in Germany, Scotland, Georgia, and Mississippi, and now makes her home in the Los Angeles area with her husband Chuck and varying numbers of children.

A former teacher, she now enjoys writing full time. Her YA novels *The Frog Princess* and *Waiting for Amanda* were winners of the RWA's Golden Medallion award. She also authored *Three's a Crowd, Star Quality, Too Many Cooks,* and *Mollie in Love* of the popular *Sisters* series.

As their boat gathered speed, the salty sea breeze tossed Stephanie's thick reddish hair.

"This is living," she murmured to herself.

Suddenly a shout reverberated across the water. Stephanie turned and saw her father waving frantically at their boat.

What could be wrong?

Then Stephanie's eyes widened and her heart began to pound wildly.

A slip speedboat, its driver's face only a pale blur, was plunging across the bay straight toward them, going so fast it seemed out of control.

"Look out!" Stephanie shrieked. She touched Eve's shoulder, pointing.

"Oh no!" Eve gasped. She clutched the wheel in a frozen grip, unable to move.

They were going to crash!

Watch for

**Tug of War**

the next book in the Smyth vs Smith
series coming soon
from Lynx!